FINDING THE LOST

FINDING THE LOST

MOOSE BEACH TRILOGY BOOK TWO

Michael Foster
Art by Gloria Miller Allen

 Z Girls Press
Sacramento, CA

Art by Gloria Miller Allen
Designed and Published by Z Girls Press
www.ZGirlsPress.com
Sacramento, California

First Edition
Copyright © 2019 by Michael Foster
www.MichaelsCabinBooks.com

Paperback ISBN-13: 978-1-7328293-5-0
Hardcover ISBN-13: 978-1-7328293-9-8
Ebook ISBN-13: 978-1-7328293-6-7

Library of Congress Control Number:2019910038

FOR MY FATHER, ROBERT,
WHO TAUGHT ME THE VALUE
OF A GOOD WALKING STICK.

"The woods are lovely, dark and deep,
But I have promises to keep,
and miles to go before I sleep."

—*Robert Frost*

"The strongest oak of the forest is not the one that is protected from the storm and hidden from the sun. It's the one that stands in the open where it is compelled to struggle for its existence against the winds and rains and the scorching sun."

—*Napoleon Hill*

CONTENTS

PROLOGUE

Alicia awoke with a start. The crackling boom of thunder rumbled through the woods outside as rain fell loudly against the roof of the small cabin she shared with her mom and dad. She listened intently, trying to understand what had disturbed her sleep. The cabin was silent except for the sound of rain and the soft snoring of Richard and Katie. What was it that had startled her awake?

The thunder came again, and with it, the faintest hint of words. "Aliiicia... cooome... daaanger... broooken... cooome fiiinnd meee!!" She strained to make out what was being said—the dark words drawn out and echoing just behind the booms. But the thunder was fading now as the storm moved on out of the lake valley.

Alicia laid her head back on the pillow. She fought to stay awake, listening, but her eyelids slowly closed with the weight of sleep. It was just her imagination, she was sure, strange dreams brought on by one too many s'mores from the night before. But as sleep began to reclaim its hold on her, her thoughts returned to that beach and adventures she had there several years ago.

CH. 1 BREAKFAST

Alicia opened her eyes to daylight coming through the window. The smell of cooked bacon hung in the air, pleasing her nose and bringing her fully awake. Lifting her head, she looked around the cabin and saw her dad tending a skillet on the wood-burning stove, the heat of which filled the cabin and chased away the chill night air.

"Good morning, sleepyhead," Richard said. "You are waking up late this morning!"

Alicia had a faint recollection of disturbing dreams that had given her a restless night. "Did you hear the thunder last night?" she asked.

Nope, I must have slept right through it," he replied.

You snored so loud, I could barely tell the difference!" she remarked. Alicia looked over at the clock, noticing it was after 11:00. "Why did you let me sleep so late? You know I need to work on my report for next week."

For Alicia, this was a vacation in name only. While the family tried to grab as much time as possible at the cabin during the summer, their visits were becoming more and more limited each year with both parents working harder than ever. Alicia herself was focused on her education and didn't have the time to explore like she used to.

Getting ready to enter high school was a big step and, during her orientation open house two weeks ago, her future English teacher had assigned an end-of-the-summer report that was supposed to describe what she had done on vacation. *It was due on the first day of class*, which meant there was homework before she had even started high school. Unbelievable!

Alicia had written similar reports when she was younger: *During my summer, I went camping with my family and caught frogs.* This one, she imagined, would have to be much more detailed. She was entering the gifted program and expected that her English teacher would want something a little more academic, especially now that she was going to be in high school.

High school, can you imagine! New students and new friends from all the different grade schools. Instead of one teacher, she would have several! She was excited to learn about advanced math and sciences. And there would be boys of course, but there was always time for that later—*much* later if her father had any say in the matter. Alicia still had her mind set on the possibility of being a botanist or a forest ranger, so it was never too early to watch her GPA and start prepping for college.

"You just looked so comfortable, I couldn't bear to disturb you," Richard said, smiling over at her. "You've been focused so much on the upcoming school year, even here at the cabin, that I thought you could use the rest."

"You're probably right," Alicia admitted. It was a Saturday, after all. But a feeling of anxiety tickled the back of her mind. "School starts in just a couple of days, though!"

The teenager loathed getting out of bed, leaving the warmth of the blankets behind. She could almost see the cold air seeping through the cracks between the logs of the cabin, spilling in like water to puddle and swirl around the floorboards. Putting on a show for her father, she crawled out of bed with loud grunts of protest and looked around the cabin.

"Where's Mom?"

"Oh, you know. With this being the last weekend we are going to spend here, she was eager to get out and enjoy the outdoors," Richard replied with a wistful look on his face. "I'm sure you can find her working on one of her drawings nearby. She already grabbed some oatmeal, so it's just you and me for breakfast."

Alicia's mom, Katie, had become quite the artist of late, and many of her sketches, drawings, and watercolors were featured in a local gallery at home. She was beginning to receive a lot of commissions for new pieces of art, and the extra work kept her busier than before, which meant less time spent here at the lake. Katie always felt more inspired from her time at the cabin than anywhere else in the world. It was common for her to run out just after daybreak to try and find the best early morning lighting for her work, when the sun's rays shone through the tree branches just so, providing a crisp color palette to work with. The nature-loving woman knew that after the rain last night, much of the dust would have settled, giving everything a cleaner, sharper appearance.

Alicia moved toward the great metal stove, arms extended in the direction of the radiating heat, and shuffled like a zombie for comedic effect. "I had the strangest dream last night," she said. "Someone was speaking to me and it felt urgent, but I can't recall their words right now."

"Too many s'mores?" her father chuckled as he watched the antics of his daughter.

"That was my exact same thought!" Alicia laughed at memories of the night before. She had been having a lot of fun making s'mores—toasting the marshmallows in the campfire and using the willow branches her dad had carved into long pointy sticks to stab the puffy white blobs and hold them close to the glowing coals. Then she would pile them on graham crackers with pieces of chocolate and smoosh them down. Her parents just sat back and watched while she ate one after the other, occasionally making one for them as well. Thinking back on it now, she was amazed at being hungry for breakfast this morning with all the sugar she'd consumed. But Alicia actually felt ravenous.

Standing in front of the stove and absorbing the warmth, Alicia reached her hands skyward and stretched up on tippy-toes for a moment, giving an exaggerated groan in the process. The teenager had grown rapidly over the past year, changing from a skinny young girl into a taller, still skinny, but athletic young woman. The growing pains she occasionally dealt with were no joke, and it always felt wonderful to stretch her muscles to the fullest as they adapted to this new body. She slowly lowered her arms and relaxed back down onto her feet, walked over to the small kitchen table, and flopped herself down onto one of the old metal chairs. She was ready for its vinyl cushion that her bare legs would stick to, anticipating the delicious bacon she'd been smelling since she awoke.

Alicia glanced at the dark purple backpack sitting propped there on the table, almost tipping over from the weight of the new textbooks inside. She couldn't believe the number of books she had to carry around. Alicia knew she would have to dig into them shortly, but for the moment she pushed the backpack hard, needing two hands to slide the heavy thing to the side to make room for the breakfast plate her dad was now carrying to the table. She could get to the report after eating.

"What'cha doin' today?" Alicia asked her dad as he set the plate down in front of her, along with a large mug of hot chocolate perfect for warming up on this chilly morning. She took a piece of bacon from her plate and dipped it into the egg yolk before taking a slow, savory bite.

"We definitely need some wood chopped for the stove," he said, sitting down across from her. "The summer's almost over, and mornings and evenings are cooling down quite a bit. I don't want to be chopping wood in the rain and snow!"

Alicia looked at her dad. He worked so hard and just cooked her breakfast. She absolutely hated the task of gathering and storing firewood, but she appreciated the food and felt she should at least offer to help. The fact that her dad would probably be calling for her in an hour anyway meant that if she volunteered first, it might earn her credit for a favor in the future. That felt like a good plan!

"If you need help stacking it later, give me a holler," she said, now dipping the half-eaten strip of bacon into her hot chocolate. "I'm sure I'll need a break from this report at some point."

"I might just do that," Richard responded, looking at his daughter like she was an alien, watching her odd eating habits. "You just take care of what you need to, my soon-to-be high schooler!"

Alicia looked up from her plate of food and saw her dad smiling at her with that all-too-familiar pride in his eyes and wondered what she had done to deserve such attention. She felt a touch of embarrassment from his gaze. Maybe it was from the fact that over the past year or so, Alicia had begun spending less and less time with her parents and more with her friends, adopting their personalities, blending them with her own. All this attention from her dad felt weird now. She was a different person than the one that would jump from her father's shoulders into the lake. The idea made her a bit sad now that she thought about it. The focused youngster used to be very active outside, exploring and playing games of make-believe. She no longer had time for make-believe, instead focusing on her education and taking it seriously. She admitted to herself there were times when she missed those adventurous days from just a few years ago.

"Your mom will help with whatever I need," her father continued. "You focus on that report."

Moving slowly, as if not wanting to be caught, Richard picked up a piece of bacon and cautiously dunked it into his coffee. Alicia pretended to be focused on her breakfast, sipping hot chocolate and peeking up as her father lifted the strip of bacon and bit off the end. He immediately made a horrible face. Alicia erupted in laughter so hard that hot chocolate flew from her nose.

"Dad!" she screamed through her laughter. Richard saw what had just happened to his daughter and began laughing himself as he watched her grab for a napkin to wipe away the cocoa running down her upper lip.

They finished their meal with small talk about the upcoming school year, smiling at each other, still giggling occasionally. Alicia glanced once again at the backpack and groaned. This was usually one of her favorite parts of the year, when the colors of the forest stopped being a uniformed green, new shades of orange and yellow added to the mix. The pollywogs had lost their tails and grown into frogs by now. There was a new batch of young squirrels collecting the last of the summer's seeds to store for the winter. She resigned herself to the fact that, as much as she wanted to get outside and explore, there was simply too much schoolwork to do, and she should have gotten started on it already.

Richard pushed his chair away and reached over the table to grab Alicia's now empty plate as well. She watched him carry the two plates into the kitchen and give everything a good rinse, knowing from experience that ants could become a nuisance if the plates were left dirty, not forgetting for a minute that the smell of food could attract bears, though usually not during the daytime.

"Thanks, Dad," Alicia said. "It was delicious. You know how to make the perfect eggs."

She loved her father, but their conversations and interactions were more infrequent as her priorities shifted. Friends were her favorite influence lately, they understood her these days more than her family did. She had never really talked with her parents about what happened three years ago during the rainstorm on that beach, how she had crossed over to the Wild Side for two whole weeks! Her father said that she had simply disappeared for about fifteen minutes. She was sure he believed it to be some imaginary game she had been playing, hiding off in the woods to give him a good scare and, in some way, she resented that! It seemed that adults never took kids seriously. She knew differently but also realized it would be impossible to convince either of her parents *what she knew* happened back then.

So she didn't bring it up anymore. Her memories of Mickey, Briar, and Fiona were starting to fade a little bit anyway.

Alicia watched as her father finished with the dishes and grabbed his jacket to go out to work in the cold morning air. Through the corner of her eye, she saw his familiar final glance in her direction as he opened the cabin door and stepped out. *I wonder who he watched before I was born,* she thought as she slid the backpack in front of her with a sigh and reached inside to take out her notebook. She settled in for a long afternoon, never knowing that she would not be helping her father stack wood that afternoon, if ever again.

CH. 2 FROZEN IN AMBER

Alicia reached for her mug, absently taking a sip before noticing that the liquid inside was now watery and cold. Most of the chocolate had already settled to the bottom. Feeling a strain in her neck, she looked up from her homework and realized she had been at it for hours. *What time was it anyway?* She had expected her dad to come in and get her when he needed help. *Now's as good a time as any to take a break.*

Standing, she stretched her back, which was cramped from being hunched over the kitchen table for what felt like hours in the same position. *Ohhh, that feels good*, she thought, rolling her shoulders and looking around the little cabin. Alicia did love this place, with its walls made of real wooden logs which were polished smooth to the touch. The old wood-burning stove was her favorite piece of furniture.

Years ago, long before she was born, a mouse had the unfortunate timing of running along one of the beams near the ceiling, right as the new cabin was settling. It had gotten its tail caught between the beam and the roof, unable to move, and with no one to hear its squeaks of despair. It died there in the rafters during the long winter. Now, decades later, the corpse of the old mouse still remained, mummified, and just far enough out of reach that removing it would be more of an effort than it was worth. Instead, and perhaps somewhat morbidly, her family left it where it was and called it the Watcher of the Cabin. Most of the time it was not visible in the darkness of the log roof crevices, but if you knew right where to look, you could spot it. The family considered it as a sort of totem or good luck charm, keeping the bad spirits away. She glanced up, spotting it hanging there along with a few remnants of old, dusty cobwebs—poor mouse.

Alicia regretted that she didn't have the time to enjoy the place as much as she wanted to this weekend. *I guess that's part of growing up,* she thought with mild regret, glancing at her textbooks. *But I suppose I should get out at least once today.*

She opened the door and stepped onto the front porch of the cabin. The rain from the night before had soaked the ground, and now, in the warm afternoon air, the scent of pine and wet dirt was rising, giving the air an earthy aroma. It was one of her favorite smells in the world—rich and damp, the same smell that emanated from digging up earthworms to use for fishing—so she took a moment to enjoy it.

The cabin and surrounding woods were a home away from home for Alicia and her family. A welcomed break from the busyness of living in a city. Here the air was fresh in a way she could almost taste. The occasional passing car or ATV would kick up clouds of dust from the dirt roads. And the night was so clear you could see billions of stars—like cream, spilled across the sky.

Located in the state of Idaho, their log cabin was set in a narrow valley in the Boise National Forest and stood on a small hill overlooking a beautiful lake. The lake was only about a mile wide and maybe two miles long, thoroughly perfect for floating on an old inner tube or paddling a kayak. When the air turned cooler and the sun began to sink behind the trees, the older folks would get in their rowboats and head to the northeast corner of the lake where the lily pads grew. It was the best spot for fly fishing, as the rainbow trout—the second thing Idaho was famous for, the first being potatoes—loved to hide beneath the wide and round floating leaves of the lilies, patiently waiting for a stray insect to buzz too close to the water. The fishermen would come home moments before it was completely dark, their wicker creels loaded with the evening's catch.

Alicia looked across the clearing behind her summer home to the neighbors' house, which was far enough away that each cabin owner had their privacy, but not so far that they were strangers. In fact, the family there had a daughter of their own who had just turned seventeen last month. Despite their age difference, their shared experiences at the lake and in the woods bonded them in friendship. That cabin stood empty now, as did many of the homes around the lake. The family staying there had been in the process of packing up and leaving for the summer just as Alicia and her parents were arriving. She barely had time to run over and give the older girl a quick hug, saying goodbye and wishing each other the best in the new school year, knowing they wouldn't see each other until next June. Over the years, Alicia had made friends with several of the children whose families owned places in the area, but it was late in the season, and almost all of the vacationers had returned to their real homes before the weather turned cold.

The rhythmic sound of chopping wood that she had heard earlier—*CHACK...thunk...CHACK... thunk*—had stopped as Alicia went to look for her mom and dad. Following the small path around the side of the cabin to where the chopping block and woodpile were, she saw no signs of her family but noticed quite a large pile of split logs and kindling waiting to be neatly stacked. *I guess they're taking a break*, she thought to herself, *or perhaps wholly distracted by the beauty of the woods or the promise of a refreshing dip in the lake.*

She circled around a large boulder at the side of the cabin. Her family nicknamed the enormous, rectangular hunk of stone Chipmunk Rock. They would place fruit rinds and peanuts on it, and the squirrels and birds would flock to snatch up the tasty treats, chattering loudly and angrily at one another. Alicia and her parents would laugh, watching the small creatures at play, and point at their curious antics. But sometimes lately, and in secret, she would look at the giant stone and remember a friend she once knew all too briefly, causing moistness to fill her eyes.

On the other side of the boulder and just beyond the edge of the woods behind the cabin, Alicia saw that her mother, had found something interesting to paint. Her dad was heading over to find out what it was and admire his wife's work. Looking at her parents, the teenager felt an unexpected surge of love race through her. Alicia knew she was lucky in more ways than she realized. The girl continued toward them, also interested in seeing what her mom was drawing.

Getting closer, she saw that her mom was completely lost in thought. Alicia could see that her concentration was so deep, Katie wasn't moving at all. Maybe her mom was drawing a squirrel or something and didn't want to make any sudden movement. She appeared to be completely frozen in place, her pencil extended toward the canvas as if she was holding her breath, waiting for precisely the right moment to begin drawing again. There was a strange shimmering in the air around her, which could simply be a trick of the light from the shadows cast by the slowly swaying tree limbs above, or moisture rising from the wet ground as it was heated by the afternoon sun. But it also triggered a faint memory in the back of Alicia's mind, one she couldn't quite latch onto at the moment.

Watching her dad approach her mom from behind, Alicia heard him calling out. "Kate?" Richard asked questioningly, softly so as not to disturb her. "Kate?" Richard reached out to gently rest his hand on his wife's shoulder, but moments before touching her, he stopped moving as well, afraid to disturb his wife's work. Alicia paused, waiting to see what was happening, but her father only stood there, his hand inches away from her mom's shoulder.

"Dad?" she inquired, walking toward them again. "Dad, what is it?"

Alicia approached her parents, both of them standing completely still. They were certainly fascinated by whatever it was they were looking at. Perhaps they were examining the source of the distortion in the air. Stepping closer, she saw the shimmering intensify for a moment and then stop as if space and light within it were holding their breath. She noticed a glint of something hovering there, surrounding her parents like sunlight on a soap bubble. A great fear clutched her stomach unexpectedly, and she rushed forward toward her parents, reaching for them and calling "Mom? Dad!"

Suddenly, her outstretched fingers slammed into... nothing! Alicia stopped, pulling back her hand and shaking off the pain. *Ouch, that hurt!* She reached out slowly with her other hand and felt a cold, curved, smooth surface where there should have been none. *What was this?* Slowly, Alicia circled her parents, keeping her hand on this bubble of air which seemed to encase her family within its cold sphere. Like insects in amber, she could see her mom and dad, eyes open, staring at nothing, unable to move, caught by something they never saw.

The fear that had begun in her stomach radiated out, raising the fine hairs on her arms and neck. Alicia slapped her hand hard against the invisible surface and felt a stinging pain in her palm. "Mom! Dad!" she shouted at them, but there was no response.

"MOM! DAD!" She screamed at the frozen bubble, slapping it over and over.

The pain in her hand finally became too much, so Alicia stopped, leaving her hand resting on the sphere, which was cool to the touch and soothing against her reddened palm. She slowly collapsed to the ground, her hand sliding down the surface of the bubble and to her mouth open in shock. She felt confusion rush in. She didn't know how this could happen. What sort of weird phenomenon was this? She had never heard of anything like it before, not ever!

Alicia felt helpless. She had watched her friend drive home only the day before and knew that most of the lake people had gone. Alicia had no one she could go to. A growing sense of panic settled into her chest, causing her heart to race.

Looking down, she began scanning the ground, her eyes finally settling on what she wanted. Alicia stretched to picked up a large jagged rock. She viciously slammed it against the invisible barrier repeatedly, once again screaming for her parents to respond. "MOM!! DAD!!" she yelled over and over, the rough edges of the stone cutting into her palm and fingers, leaving red streaks on the rock and the clear bubble encasing her parents.

Alicia sobbed filled with frustration and confusion, pounding the stone, pounding, pounding against the barrier. What sort of magic was this?

Magic.

Suddenly, she paused in her bashing, and her thoughts flew back to the events of three years ago. Magic! She didn't know what this was. She didn't know how to free her parents. But she remembered. And she knew one place where she might find an answer.

CH. 3 PREPARATIONS

Alicia arose from where she collapsed at the base of the bubble. She looked at her frozen parents for another moment, turned, tossed the bloody rock aside, then ran to the cabin. Flinging open the door, Alicia moved swiftly to the kitchen table and grabbed her backpack, upending it on the table, and dumped a variety of pens, pencils, erasers, books, and papers onto the Formica surface with a clatter. Focused on the task at hand, she ignored several items that bounced to the floor, took the now empty backpack and scanned the interior of the small cabin with determination. There would be no more traveling the wilds with simply a bathing suit and a towel! This time, she had every intention to be better prepared before crossing, if that was even a possibility.

Alicia quickly built a mental checklist: food, water, flashlight, blanket, and knife. She had no idea how long her journey might take, but she wanted to make sure she had all the necessities. Alicia knew she could scavenge for food and water. After all, she had already spent a long time in the Wild Side during her last visit, and her friends there had taught her so much, but it was good to have emergency rations just in case. "Fortune favors the prepared mind," her dad liked to quote.

Her friends! Would she see Mickey, Fiona, and Briar again? A squirrel, a deer, and a jaybird were the most unusual trio of companions one could ever ask for. A brief moment of excitement flared inside her at the thought as a smile touched her lips, but it was quickly erased by a glance out of the dusty cabin window and at the sight of her parents trapped there, beyond the edge of the forest. *What had caused this?* A renewed sense of urgency overcame the girl, and she set her mind to the task of gathering essentials.

Alicia quickly dressed, having never changed out of her pajamas and slippers since getting out of bed. She yanked on a pair of jeans and dug through her suitcase which remained unpacked since their arrival the previous day. Alicia pulled on a t-shirt and light jacket, which should be enough to protect her from branches that might scratch her bare arms as she moved through the woods. Finally, she sat down on the wooden floor and slid her feet into long socks and hiking boots. The shoes were a bit old now and pinched her toes due to a growth spurt she went through earlier in the summer, but they were all she had. She would be going into high school quite a bit taller than she had left eighth grade, so her mom had planned to take her shopping for new clothes as soon as they got back home from the cabin.

Standing, Alicia grabbed a thin but warm blanket from the bed and stuffed it down into the depths of the backpack. She went to the cabinet and took out a flashlight and a small folding pocket knife. The flashlight went into the pack and the knife was tucked into the front pocket of her jeans. Having noticed a large box of wooden matches on the cabinet shelf, she grabbed those as well, knowing she wanted to be able to make a fire in the evenings. There was a large package of beef jerky on the counter as well as a bag of homemade trail mix—"gorp" as her family called it— and both went into the pack. Lastly, she grabbed her Thermos, filling it from the sink, cold water splashing onto her fingers in her haste. She then slid the full container into a pouch on the side of the backpack.

Alicia gathered a piece of paper from the table and a pencil from where it had rolled off onto the floor. She hastily scribbled out a note to her parents:

IF YOU SEE THIS AND WONDER WHERE I AM, DON'T WORRY. I WENT OVER TO MOOSE BEACH FOR A LITTLE HIKE. I'LL BE BACK SOON.

LOVE, *LISH*

She left it on the countertop, plainly visible to anyone who walked in.

A mental tally and final glance around the cabin assured her she hadn't forgotten anything. She put her arms through the loops of the backpack and, cinching the straps tight, stepped out the door and onto the trail toward the lake.

Alicia slowed as she walked past her mom and dad, stopping to look at them again. She approached the not-quite-visible bubble, with the sun glinting off the surface, and spoke softly.

"I'm going. I have to find an answer, and I...I think I know where to look. Please don't worry about me. I'll be safe, I promise." Who knew if they even *could* worry? Maybe they could hear her, maybe not.

Looking at them, seeing them in this way, was surreal. Her father's eyes were open wide and she could see the blue-green color of the irises. His eyes looked like two shiny marbles. Alicia had seen taxidermy work before, a stuffed raccoon in a roadside convenience store, or the head of a deer on the wall of one of her parents' friend's houses. Seeing her father this way reminded her of it, and she shuddered at the thought of her parents stuffed and mounted.

"I'll be back as soon as I can," she promised. "I'm sure we can fix this."

In truth, she didn't feel sure at all, but the words felt necessary, if not for her parents, then for her to speak them out loud. A robin sang in a nearby tree, and the happiness in its voice did not match the deep sadness Alicia felt.

"I love you both, and I'll see you soon."

With that, she turned away and headed toward the lake path. The determined girl walked quickly to the small slope and looked down the hill at her dock and the rowboat tied to the shore. Moving carefully, she descended the slope.

As she walked down the path, Alicia glanced toward the trees lining the trail on her right and came to an abrupt halt, staring at what she saw. Another glint hung in the air next to one of the trees. On the surface of the large pine were two red squirrels paused in mid-chase, frozen exactly like her parents. The girl stepped toward the tree and reached her hand out gingerly, feeling the familiar coldness of the invisible sphere. *Oh, my gosh, it was here too!* She hurried back to the path, unease growing within her, and continued down to the lake and the waiting boat. If it was here as well, how many more places was this happening?

Reaching the lake, Alicia stepped up to the tree stump where the rowboat was tied. The old boat, painted green and yellow, rocked gently on the small waves. She untied the knot and slowly pulled the boat along with her as she stepped out from the shore and onto the wooden dock. She stared across the lake, picking out the recognizable shape of Moose Beach along the far shoreline. It was her destination.

Alicia dragged the boat to the front of the dock and knelt alongside it, feeling the wood grain of the dock's hard boards digging into her knees. She pulled off her backpack, placed it on the floorboards of the boat, and grabbed a life jacket from where it lay discarded on the seat. Pulling on the life jacket, she buckled it tightly around her chest. Alicia was a good swimmer, having learned here in this very lake, but it was never wise to overestimate one's ability. If she were to capsize the boat in the middle of the lake, she wasn't confident that she would have the strength to be able to swim all the way to shore.

Alicia gently put one leg over the side of the boat and firmly rested it on the floorboards, gaining her balance before stepping in with the other leg and taking a seat on the bench in the middle of the boat. She pushed away from the dock, lifted one of the oars from where it was stored along the inside wall of the boat, and fitted it snuggly into the oarlock. She did the same for the other side, sat up straight, taking one oar in each hand. She had been practicing rowing over the past couple of years with her dad and, as a result of her recent growth spurt, her arms were even longer and more easily able to manage the oars on either side. She was endlessly amused by the fact that the rower sat backward in the boat, facing the rear, basically paddling in reverse the whole time. This amusing thought broke the tension of the moment—worried for her parents and for herself—Alicia knew what she had to do.

Pushing down on the handles, she leaned forward, forcing the blades of the oars into the air behind her. A light breeze danced across her cheeks, making her hair flutter before traveling onward in the direction of the far shore. *Good*, she thought. *That breeze will help with the rowing.* As she lifted her arms, the paddles sunk into the water, so she pulled back hard, feeling her muscles tighten as the oars fought the resistance of the water, making the little boat move slowly backward Looking over her shoulder, she adjusted her aim a bit, getting the front of the boat pointed toward the proper spot on the far shore and repeated the motion, digging in again with the oars, the resistance somewhat diminished thanks to the momentum she was building.

It would take about fifteen minutes to cross the lake. Alicia fell into a rhythm—push down, lean forward, raise up, pull back—over and over again, letting her mind drift. She didn't know what to expect when she got to the other side, but memories of her first visit to the Wild Side came back, and she started to form a plan.

CH. 4 THE JOURNEY BEGINS

Alicia reached the opposite side of the lake with little incident. Looking to her left and right as she rowed, unusual but familiar glints glistened in the air far in the distance. At one point, she passed an osprey trapped in mid-flight, a fish stiffly clutched in his sharp talons. Whatever was happening, it was widespread. She heard the beating in her chest above the sounds of nature—these sights terrified her. Was this happening only here at her lake, close to the barrier of the other realm? Or had it spread much farther, outside these woods and to the cities beyond? Was her English teacher, instead of thinking about the new school year and the reports she would soon be grading, sitting locked in place at her table with a coffee cup raised, prepared to take a drink that never came? Gooseflesh raised on her arms at the thought.

Reaching the other side of the lake, Alicia stopped rowing and let the last bit of momentum carry the boat gently to the shore. She allowed the tip to bump up against the reeds and grass of the shoreline before taking action. Moving swiftly, she tied the boat to the same fallen tree her father had tied the boat to three years earlier and hung a rubber bumper over each side of the boat as protection against knocking into the log and rocks.

After stepping out with the same care that she entered the boat, Alicia took off her life jacket and tossed it back onto the floorboards. Standing on the beach with her hands on her hips, she studied the forest in front of her. It didn't look different than any other section of woods that she had seen a million times in her life here at the lake, but she knew deep down that it was. She had been back to this beach on several occasions with her parents since the events of three years ago, but had never returned to the

Wild Side. This time would be different. Equal parts excitement and trepidation filled her.

Alicia let her mind go back to when she was eleven years old. What had she done? She remembered watching her father messing with the boat and then seeing something out of the corner of her eye that distracted her. What had it been? She'd tried to focus on some barely-seen movement and couldn't seem to get it into focus. Every time her eyes darted in the direction, it would vanish and appear elsewhere. *That's right! My eyes!* She had to let her eyes go out of focus. She had looked beyond!

Reaching back toward the rowboat, Alicia grabbed her backpack and strapped it on. She turned once more to face the forest. "Okay, let's do this," she said to herself and stared into the shadows beyond the edge, letting her eyes relax. Looking into the distance, she saw... nothing. The darkness of the shadows remained simply that—dark. Nothing happened.

Oh NO! she thought. *What if I can't go back?!* She stared harder, trying to let her mind wander so that her eyes could remain unfocused, but it was impossible.

"AAARRGGGHHH!!" Alicia screamed in frustration, startling a group of orioles gathered in a nearby bush into flight. What was she supposed to do now? This was her only hope; the only idea she came up with for trying to save her parents. Was she supposed to go back, wait, and do nothing but hope that things got better?

Alicia felt beads of sweat trickle down the back of her neck while she struggled to come up with a solution. Perhaps she could try to row to the lodge and seek help there, but what if they were frozen, too? No, the answers *had* to be on the Wild Side. How could this happen to her, to her parents? It wasn't fair! Hadn't she already rescued that stupid realm? And now this?! She seethed at the injustice of it all.

"No, I *will not* give up!" she shouted into her frozen surroundings. Focusing all of the frustration inside of her, she stared once again into the forest, fists balled at her side, and let her eyes go soft.

Suddenly, like a blurry image coming into focus under a microscope, the world *snapped* into clarity. She saw it! Alicia stepped forward and in.

A tingle rushed through her body, racing down her arms and legs as if the largest goose in the world had walked over her grave. The feeling held for a moment, almost painful in its intensity, raising the hairs on her arms and neck underneath her jacket, and then slowly fading away.

How strange, she thought, shaking her arms as if to fling off the last of the goosebumps.

She paused and took a moment to look around the woods, noticing once again the intensity of the colors in the Wild Side, how deep the greens and reds appeared here, how bright and sunny the yellows. The air felt significantly warmer and smelled cleaner here too, which made a sort of sense considering the lack of factories and vehicles belching out smoke into the air.

She looked deeply into the forest for any sign of her friends, but no one was around. A profound sense of disappointment crept into her chest, but she angrily banished it.

"What did I expect," she asked out loud, "a welcoming party?"

Of course, they would not simply be waiting here, that was a silly thought. Nobody knew she was coming, but as she stepped farther into the realm, her eyes continued to watch for familiar faces.

It all looked so different! Though only three years had passed, everything appeared overgrown. Clearly, the release of Gran'Tree's water during her last visit had a tremendous effect on the vegetation in the Wild Side.

Alicia glanced behind her and saw that the lake was still there. The last time she was here, a meadow stretched out as far as the eye could see. However, now she saw the sparkling blue water right where it belonged, though she could no longer see her cabin on the other side. There was still a shimmer in the air though, right where she had stepped through. Strange, it hadn't been there the last time she came here.

Alicia paused to get her bearings. She had already formed a loose plan in her mind during the trip across the lake. She remembered Mickey telling her about how the barrier between the worlds formed so long ago. He had talked of the great Ancient Ones—Thunderbolt, Vulcan, and the Silver King—all coming together and using their combined power to separate the realms of mankind and magic. Based on their descriptions, she recognized them all as physical locations in her world. Thunderbolt was a tall mountain to the north, Vulcan was a large clearing filled with hot springs to the southwest, and even further south was the old Eureka Silver King Mine. Surely that could not all be a coincidence. Considering that it must have taken tremendous magic to create the barrier, Alicia believed that one of the Ancients would understand the magic at work back home and have the solution to free her parents.

She decided that she should start by going to Thunderbolt. The mountain of the same name was the highest peak in the area, towering over the lands and she imagined that, just like Zeus on Mount Olympus, the being there must watch over everything. She recalled that Mickey had said it was actually the Silver King who was the strongest of the Ancient Ones. But Thunderbolt was the closest, and Alicia was determined to find a solution quickly and get back home to her parents. She had no idea what the long term effects of being frozen in a bubble might be, but it couldn't be good, so that settled it. She would make the mountain her first destination.

Alicia surveyed the ground quickly looking for a good walking stick—a must-have for any hike. She spotted a dead, fallen tree close by. Walking over to it, she grabbed one of the long branches sticking out and pulled hard. With a loud snap, it separated from the tree trunk. Alicia picked up a stone and ran it up and down along the upper section of the branch, removing any extra pokey bits and creating a smooth spot to grip.

With her pack strapped tightly to her back and walking stick in hand, Alicia glanced one more time at the lake and across the water to where her cabin existed in her world. Using the large body of water as a point of reference, she set herself due north and headed out, picking the way through the overgrowth, her eyes searching for a trail to ease the passage.

As Alicia walked, she continued to look around, hoping to see her squirrel friend come bounding through the brush, or hear Briar's familiar "CAW! CAW!" as he swooped down from the treetops. However, there was nothing but the regular sounds of the forest: the wind through the branches above, the chirping of birds, and the quiet susurrus of hidden insects.

Why am I thinking this way? Alicia asked herself. *Talking squirrels and telepathic deer? Of course they aren't here. They are off living their animal lives, moved on the same as I have.* She scolded herself through her thoughts. *I'm not eleven anymore, geesh! Let's forget about that and focus on what's important. First, I've gotta get up that darned mountain. Then I have to get home and rescue Mom and Dad. And finally, I've got to finish that blasted report before school next week!* She laughed unexpectedly. "I sure am going to have a story to tell about my summer vacation!" she blurted out loud. The insect sounds paused briefly with the outburst of noise, then resumed their whisper of music.

"I only hope there is a school to go back to," she said, talking to herself and thinking about how many of the strange frozen bubbles she had seen. She wondered how far this epidemic had spread.

CH. 5 CHILDHOOD LOST

Alicia quickly discovered that the hike was much more challenging than expected, with many fallen trees, great tangles of bushes everywhere, and no clear path. She had to clamber over rotted logs and through tall brush that snagged her hair, which slowed progress significantly. She hoped that she could get at least close, if not all the way, to the base of Thunderbolt before nightfall, but it didn't look like she'd be able to make it now.

The girl stopped for a moment to catch her breath and survey the surroundings. She could not believe the amount of growth in the three years since her first visit to the Wild Side. The last time she had been here—the only time actually—the lands were starved for water thanks to the great tree that had chosen to steal all the rain for himself. During the time her friends called "The Drying," it was dusty, with little undergrowth to tangle her feet.

But now it looked practically prehistoric! The colors were rich, deep browns and greens, and massive ferns dotted the landscape. The water that Gran'Tree released certainly caused quite the growth spurt. Perhaps the moisture absorbed some of the yellow pine's magic while it was stored inside the great tree and was now passing along that magic to the plants that absorbed it.

Alicia chuckled. *I went through the same growth spurt myself over the past three years. Maybe there's magic in me too! I do remember Bristleback and Gran'Tree saying they saw something magical in me. But I've never felt anything.*

While resting, she let her mind drift back to thoughts of Bristleback, the enormous mountain troll. Alicia only knew him for such a short time, but she and the very old, misunderstood creature had bonded quickly through the shared loss of family.

His death came far too suddenly, but his passing had given her the strength to meet Gran'Tree and demand a change. Bristleback's stony remains at the edge of the great tree's clearing, clear proof of what the yellow pine had done to the lands, forced Gran'Tree to face the truth of his ways. In the end, Alicia believed that the mountain troll's death had helped save them all and helped her find the way home. Three years later, she still felt the onset of tears when thinking about her old friend.

She pushed thoughts aside to focus more intently on the task at hand—getting through the darn bushes to finding a trail! With a groan, Alicia resumed her trek using the walking stick like a machete, slashing at bushes and swiping away the branches from fallen trees so she could pass without getting scratched. She frequently glanced to the west to keep her bearings, and seeing the twinkling glint of the sun off the lake confirmed that she was still on track. The trees were too densely packed in this section of the woods eliminating a clear line of sight to the mountain which was her destination, so the determined hiker relied on the lake for directions.

Alicia noted that she had not seen any of the bubbles of frozen time here in the Wild Side. Did that mean the phenomenon only affected her world? Did the magic here prevent it from happening? She didn't have the answer, but she hoped the Ancient One she traveled to see would have one.

"Oh please, oh please, let this work," she pleaded, talking out loud to keep herself company and hoping that, maybe, her words would be heard by whatever powers existed in this realm.

She continued trudging through the brush and looking off in the distance for any telltale signs of a trail. As she walked, Alicia became acutely aware of how much more noise the forest made here than it did at home, even more than the last time she was here. The absence of humans in this world of magic allowed the wild creatures to flourish. The sounds of bugs and birdsong filled the air along with some other unidentifiable squeals and whistles. It was almost like listening to an orchestra tune their instruments before performing, a beautiful cacophony of noises that you could get lost in.

A handsome robin landed on a nearby branch, and Alicia paused to watch it. The bird's dark wings and reddish-orange breast looked beautiful, so she spoke to him.

"Hello, Mr. Robin," she said sweetly. "It's a beautiful day, isn't it?"

The bird only watched the girl with curiosity, his small black eyes were focused on the stranger, inquisitive, but he didn't respond. After a moment, the bird flitted its wings and flew off toward another branch; its eyes ever watchful for bugs or caterpillars to eat.

"Well, I guess that one doesn't speak," she said glumly.

Come to think of it, she heard the noises of small creatures scuttling through the bushes, and maybe even something larger moving close by, yet unseen, but none of the animals had come to see her. They may feel curious about her, but they did not attempt to communicate. Could her companions from three years ago have been an anomaly? She assumed, perhaps incorrectly, that most all the denizens of the forest could speak.

Alicia paused with a horrible thought passing through her head. Maybe none of them had talked—her friends from before. Could it have been like when she played with dolls as a young child, making up unique voices for each one? After all, she had participated in many back and forth conversations with her favorite toys when she was little. And she had firmly believed they were all alive in their own ways. But, those were merely childish games—right? She knew better now. *I am almost in high school!* she thought. There is no room for make-believe anymore. Could she have imagined the conversations of three years ago? The thought saddened her deeply.

"Maybe this is part of growing up," she mused with more than a touch of sorrow, speaking aloud as if that would help convince her of this truth. "Maybe letting go of the magic of childhood and the childish things that go along with it is a necessary step on the path to becoming an adult."

Alicia resisted that idea. She felt excited to grow up—she really did! And couldn't wait to get to high school and get to know her new teachers, make new friends, and maybe even meet a nice boy! Isn't that what happens in High School? But, she also did not want to lose the magic she felt at the cabin. Perhaps it was inevitable, but she made a promise to herself, right then and there, that no matter what, she would always hold onto her memories of when she was young, when the world had been a mystery just waiting to be explored.

Alicia returned her attention to the hike and fell into a sort of trance. *Whack bushes, break branches, step over logs, repeat.* Her long legs made it easy for her to navigate over all the fallen detritus that lay strewn across the forest floor. Just three years ago, she would have had to make more of an effort climbing up and over some of the logs that she now easily cleared with a jump. With the rhythm established, she increased her speed a bit, though she still wished for some sort of trail to follow.

The sun began to drop below the tree line on the opposite side of the lake. It was that time of the evening when the wind suddenly decided to stop as if holding its breath before the onset of darkness. Even though she still had quite a bit of time left before nightfall, Alicia decided to make camp now while there was still daylight. Looking around, she found a nearby spot that had less vegetation and a little more space. She set about clearing the area of as much debris as possible. Wanting to build a small campfire, it was particularly important to remove any dead branches and pine needles.

Sloughing off her backpack, she placed it on the ground and began searching the area scanning for something specific. Spotting what she was looking for, the teenager walked a few yards away and picked up a long branch that still had several patches of green pine needles on it. It had most likely broken from its tree during a windstorm, or perhaps a bear had climbed a pine and had snapped off the branch with the weight of its claws. Returning to the clearing, she used the branch almost like a broom, sweeping away combustible material from the ground and creating a nice empty space in the center.

With that task completed, Alicia went about the business of collecting stones, the bigger they were, the better. These she set in a small circle about two feet in diameter, then continued piling stones until she had created a nice barrier. Digging into her pocket, she pulled out the knife she had tucked away there. Alicia repeatedly stabbed the knife into the ground in the center of the stones, loosening the soil and scooped the dirt out, forming a shallow pit within the circle of stones. Once she finished, Alicia put the knife back in her pocket and collected handfuls of the dead pine needles and some of the sticks she had swept away, piling them loosely in the center of the pit—needles on the bottom, sticks on top. Finally, she gathered a collection of assorted dead branches to use as logs for her fire. These she piled nearby, close enough that she would not have to search for them in the dark, but far enough away to remove any danger of sparks or coals popping out of the fire and burning them. As she did this, Alicia remembered her previous trek when she and her furry friends piled into small caverns, huddling together for warmth. Now she was on a mission for answers to save her parents, so she was prepared, unlike the first time she stumbled into the Wild Side.

Alicia knelt and dug into her backpack, pulling out the bags of trail mix and beef jerky. She had a good amount of each but, considering her options and glancing toward the lake; another idea popped into her head. She stuffed the food back into the pack and went in search of a long, sharp stick. Finding a nice heavy one about three feet in length, she came back to the clearing, sat down, and pulled out the pocketknife once again. Holding the stick firmly in one hand, she slid the knife blade down toward the end, slicing the wood in small strokes away from her as she rotated the stick until she had a nice pointy tip. Alicia stood and hefted the crude spear in one hand, testing its balance and weight. At that moment, she felt like she belonged in this prehistoric world and was going to feast on fish for dinner!

Alicia sat close to the small campfire she had made, holding her fish over the flames using a thick willow branch she carved as a skewer. She'd spent almost an hour trying to hunt fish with her makeshift spear, thrusting it into the water near the shoreline and missing several times. Night was falling, and she worried that the encroaching darkness would make it impossible to see, but eventually, her efforts paid off, and she looked forward to the trout that had nearly finished cooking.

Fully dark now, the sunlight and accompanying birdsong gave way to shadows as well as an increase in the volume of insect noise. It seemed the bugs instinctively knew that their predators had gone to sleep for the evening, so they felt safe enough to sing their unique songs. The chirping crickets were the loudest, creating a perfectly consistent tempo for the rest of the "band" to follow along.

The moon was still a few days away from being full, so she couldn't see much beyond the reach of the firelight and the edge of the clearing that she had created. However, she could hear small noises just outside her range of vision. Alicia knew nocturnal creatures, like flying squirrels and mice, would be out scavenging for seeds and grubs at this hour.

Staring off into the darkness of the woods, Alicia saw small lights in the distance that she had never seen before. They'd flick on and hover like hummingbirds, then dart quickly away. They were too far, and it was too dark for her to be able to identify them, but thought they looked a bit like fireflies. The truth is, she hadn't seen fireflies in real life, only in books. Because of her love of folklore, she had also read about will-o'-the-wisps, phantom lights that could lure unsuspecting travelers to their deaths. Even though she didn't believe the tales, Alicia decided it would be best not to investigate the lights, choosing instead to focus on cooking dinner. She had no idea what was possible in the Wild Side.

Her love of the outdoors meant that she was not afraid of the dark and never had been for that matter, having spent plenty of time outside at night with her parents, going on short hikes with their flashlights, or laying on the dock, looking up at the stars. The night sky looked amazing this far removed from the lights of the city, with the Milky Way clearly visible. In August, the Perseid meteor shower filled the sky with shooting stars.

One of her favorite nighttime activities was walking the trail to Aunt Molly's hot springs by the river near their cabin. At some point in the past, campers hauled in old bathtubs and placed them near the springs to catch the natural thermal water that boiled out of the rocks on the side of a hill before flowing down to join the river. The water directly from the rocks was too hot to touch, but you could walk to the river with a bucket, scoop up the cold water there, carry it back to the tubs and dump it in to bring the temperature down to the perfect level for soaking. The steam would rise, billowing into the sky, and if you were quiet and lucky, a young fawn might wander by while you were enjoying the warm bath.

Her fish was almost ready, so Alicia rested the skewer between two of the stones at the edge of the fire, digging the handle end of the stick into the soft dirt so that it wouldn't tip over and drop her meal into the coals. She turned and grabbed her backpack, removing the knife from the front pocket where she had stored it after carving the cooking stick.

Flipping open the pocketknife, she turned back toward the campfire and froze, her breath caught in her throat. Staring at her from the dark of the woods on the opposite side of the flames were two eyes, the deepest shade of gold that she had ever seen. Alicia couldn't move, she couldn't think. All she could do was stare at those eyes, hovering a few feet above the ground. The golden eyes held hers, unblinking, firelight reflecting off their surface. All the sounds of the woods seemed to have stopped, and the lights she had seen dancing through the trees were no longer visible. A silence that settled over her camp was almost deafening. Only the wind, which had re-awakened with the setting of the sun, had a voice.

As she watched, a huge paw came into view from the bushes. Despite the heat from the fire, Alicia suddenly felt chilled as if she had been doused in icy water. From out of the darkness of the forest stepped an enormous cougar.

And it looked hungry.

CH. 6 TAWNY

The massive cat stepped fully into the firelight, and Alicia could see the size of the beast. An all-consuming terror gripped her; she could not move—frozen in place like her parents encapsulated in the bubble. The cat was as big as her neighbor's Saint Bernard but had vastly longer and sharper teeth that gleamed now in the firelight.

She tore her gaze from the cat's and locked on its paws the size of dinner plates, with the pointed tips of claws poking out from beneath the dirty fur that covered them. She knew those claws could rip the flesh of her belly open with one swipe, allowing the beast to feed on her intestines while she lay bleeding out in the dirt.

Alicia clutched the small pocketknife, the only defense she had, tightly in her hand. It was small and perfect for cutting open fish or sharpening sticks, but not ideal for fighting. Alicia knew that, but her self-protection instinct was on high alert holding the knife and ready to use it.

She looked once again at the cougar's face and could see her image reflected in the bright yellow eyes facing her. The cat stood on the opposite side of the fire and continued to watch her hungrily; its gaze never wavering. Alicia felt paralyzed under that golden stare, as surely as if the creature standing before her was Medusa, the monster from Greek mythology with a head covered in snakes. Medusa turned unwitting adventurers to stone with just a look.

After an excruciatingly long moment, the cougar looked away from the petrified girl, glancing instead toward the fish propped up against the rocks surrounding the campfire. Once their eye contact broke, Alicia felt the hypnotizing feeling fall away slightly, but she remained still, assessing the situation with every sense of her being. Oh, how she longed for the protection of Bristleback right now. But the troll was long gone, succumbed to the effects of The Drying. She would have to find a solution and save herself.

Reaching slowly forward, questing for the branch with one hand while never taking her eyes off of the mountain lion, Alicia withdrew her cooking stick from the fire. She set the knife down at her side to indicate she was no threat, but kept it within quick reach just in case. Ever so slowly, she extended the cooked fish out toward the great cat, the stick held tightly in her hand trembling she tried hard to remain steady, hoping the golden-eyed cat understood her gesture of friendship. She remembered from her previous visit to the Wild Side that not everything should be taken at face value—what at first might appear to be the greatest threat could become your most steadfast ally.

The cougar watched her, its tawny eyes flicking between her face and the trout she offered. Was it considering her as a meal rather than the small fish she presented? The cold in her blood had faded, now replaced with a rush of adrenaline that had her skin covered in beads of sweat which shone in the firelight as her arm fully extended to the cat. She held that position, the arm quivering from both the weight of the fish as well as from fear.

For a moment, the cougar held perfectly still. Then, quick as a flash, it lunged forward, snapping the fish from the tip of the stick, its huge jaws coming together with a loud *clack!* Alicia felt a rush of hot breath from the creature. Frightened by the swiftness of the attack, she fell backward in her haste to get away. Scrambling to get control of herself, Alicia faced the beast on her hands and knees, tears streaming down her cheeks revealing her fear.

The cougar watched her again for a moment, looking unconcerned, the cooked fish held firmly by its sharp teeth. Alicia, frozen in place, glanced at the knife that had fallen just out of reach. Looking back at the beast, she wiped at the tears on her face with the back of one hand, trying to remain strong, and failing.

With a flick of its tail, the great cat turned and walked slowly into the trees, without so much as a glance back at the cowering, frightened girl. Alicia watched as the darkness swallowed the powerful shape, and the cougar disappeared as quickly as it had arrived.

She let out a gasp, unaware that she had been holding her breath, as her body still trembled in the heat from the fire. The flames were dying, so she threw in another branch to bring the campfire back to life, but the warmth could not dispel the cold that came from within, causing her to shiver uncontrollably. Alicia had no more food to cook and no appetite for eating anyway.

Staring in the direction of the cougar, even though there was nothing left to see, Alicia was grateful she had survived. She was still shaking and terrified, but she survived! Somewhere in the back of her mind, she had known there were cougars in these mountains, but in her young life, she had never seen one—until now.

And I survived!

Alicia pulled her backpack closer to the fire, removed the blanket from within, and laid down on her side. Using the pack as a pillow, she stretched the blanket over her curled body and watched as the flames slowly danced until they died down. As the flood of adrenaline left her system, an immense tiredness settled over her, but she would not sleep tonight. Of that, she was sure.

She planned to reach Thunderbolt tomorrow. For all its beauty, the Wild Side held dangers too. Alicia was well aware of that before making the decision which brought her to this moment, but she wished more than ever on this cold night alone, to be home with her parents in the comfort and safety of the cabin. Despite the brave thoughts and confidence that got her to the Wild Side and saved her life this evening, she was ready for this adventure to end and for her life to get back to normal. Without realizing it, she closed her eyes and the soft weight of sleep took her.

Alicia slowly opened her eyes and saw light filtering through the pine branches. It was daytime, and the world around her shone bright and green, so many shades of green. Slowly she sat up, the blanket falling to her lap, and looked around the clearing. The fire died in the night, and the campsite remained empty with no sign of the cat.

She didn't know how long she stayed awake after the cougar left, but, clearly, she had been wrong about not being able to sleep. She wasn't aware of falling asleep at all, but the tension of the moment last night exhausted her so completely that she was unable to keep her eyes open. She recalled listening for any telltale sounds of the cat's return but noticed the insect songs were back, and the next thing she knew, the sun woke her as it rose on the horizon.

Alicia clambered to her feet and reached her arms up with a groan, feeling the stretch of muscles along her back and legs. The teenager was athletic and enjoyed playing soccer in school, along with other activities in P.E., so she wasn't sore at all from yesterday's hike. However, the stress from the previous night's encounter along with sleeping on the ground had made her muscles stiffen up, and it felt good to stretch them out.

She was starving this morning but did not want to take the time to try fishing again, so she dug into the pack and pulled out her food supplies. Alicia stuffed a fat piece of beef jerky into her mouth and chewed. She also poured out a small amount of the gorp, made of assorted nuts combined with raisins, pieces of pineapple, and a few chocolate chips, into her hand. Once she had thoroughly chewed and swallowed the jerky, she snacked slowly on the tasty mix which would have to sustain her until lunchtime. She hoped to find some huckleberries along the way as well, but so far, she had not noticed any berry bushes at all.

Alicia picked up her blanket and vigorously shook it off, trying to remove as much dirt as possible. She stuffed it into the backpack, putting the bags of foodstuffs on top for easy access. With a yawn and another stretch, she reached down and picked up her backpack, strapping it on and cinching it tight. She was ready for whatever today had in store.

Before leaving, she checked the fire using her walking stick to stir the ashes. There were no live coals that she could see, and holding her hand a few inches above the pit she felt no residual heat. Nevertheless, Alicia buried any remaining bits of coal, knowing that last thing she needed on this adventure was a wildfire! Her mouth was dry and parched so she pulled the water bottle from her pack and took a long drink, then dumped half of the remaining contents slowly over the pit, knowing she could always find a stream to fill the bottle again. Finally, she covered everything with the stones that she had collected for the rim to be safe.

The woods were precious to all who enjoyed them, and Richard's campfire safety techniques were ingrained in the teenager's mind, even though all signs of the drought she experienced in the Wild Side three years ago were gone, replaced by lush, healthy vegetation.

Satisfied that the fire was out, Alicia picked up the spear she had carved and slid it through the tops of the straps of her backpack, trapping it snuggly against her shoulder blades. It would make travel a bit more difficult, as she would have to be aware of how wide the ends stuck out from her sides, but she didn't want to go through the process of having to carve another one. Though she forgot about it completely last night when the cougar appeared, in an emergency, she could certainly use the spear as a weapon, but sincerely hoped it didn't come to that.

Grabbing her walking stick, Alicia headed north once again toward the mountain and, hopefully, toward some answers. As she walked, she surveyed the surroundings a little more frequently, her eyes peeled for any sign of the golden-eyed cat from last night. There was nothing to be seen, though she frequently heard sounds of movement in the bushes when there didn't seem to be any wind blowing. Was her imagination playing tricks on her, or was the cougar stalking her, waiting for an opportunity to pounce, or steal another fish? Alicia recalled that humans are not supposed to feed bears, or any wild animals for that matter—it makes them less afraid, seeing people as a source of food once they've been fed. Alicia didn't know if large cats reacted the same way, but she did increase her pace a little, just in case the large cat now saw her as a meal service.

After a couple of hours of travel, the sound of flowing water filled the air and seemed to be coming from the east. Alicia decided to travel in that direction, moving away from the sight of the lake. Following the burbling sound, she soon located a small stream hidden beneath reddish, leafy bushes that lined its banks. On the opposite side of the stream, she found a cleared trail she had been hoping to find since arriving in the Wild Side. Clearly, this stream provided a regular water source for the local fauna as the trail came right to the water's edge before wandering off toward the north. While not very wide, the path was perfect for her needs.

Alicia leaned over the stream, cupped her hands under the clear, cool water, and drank the refreshing, cold liquid while water sloshed through her fingers and down the sides of her cheeks, wetting her shirt. She didn't care. The day was warm and the dampness felt good against her skin. She drank enough to slake her thirst before dipping her bottle into the stream, allowing it to fill to overflowing, then replacing it in her backpack.

Leaping nimbly across the small stream, she walked the few steps to the main trail. Looking in the direction of her destination, the mountain, Alicia saw that the trail went the same way, more or less. Knowing from experience that she would most likely find some berry bushes along the path as well, she hoped the animals had left her enough sweet fruit for a meal. She wanted to conserve the food she had brought with her for as long as possible.

The trail was easy to walk on. The ground retained just enough residual moisture from the most recent rainfall to make it soft, and a bit spongy, which was so unlike the dry, hard soil of her previous visit. Her speed of travel increased significantly, and Alicia felt confident that she would reach the mountain before nightfall.

As the morning turned to afternoon, the temperature continued to rise, though occasionally, Alicia would pass through odd pockets of cold air—places that were more sheltered from the sun and wind where the cool air of the night lingered along with the darkness, refusing to give up its hold to the sun's relentless demands. In these patches of space, bumps would rise along her exposed arms, as a small shiver passed through her.

Thoughts of her parents ever-present in the back of her mind would come to her in these moments, and she wondered if they felt anything. *Are they aware of what is happening? Are their minds still active while they're frozen in that bubble? Are they cold?* She remembered attending the funeral of a great aunt once, someone that she had barely known, and having similar questions about her deceased relative. These thoughts spurred her footsteps, and she picked up her pace. Alicia didn't know if she had to race against the clock to save them, but if there was any chance at all that they were suffering, she needed to find an answer as quickly as possible.

The early afternoon passed steadily and without incident. The trail she followed bisected similar paths, but the determined hiker continued heading north toward her goal. As expected, she did find several huckleberry bushes along the way, allowing her to take short breaks every couple of hours to stuff her face with the sweet, purple goodies.

Alicia continued to look for her friends but found no sign of them—honestly, could she expect anything else? The forest was a vast place. Mickey, Briar, and Fiona could be miles and miles away. She didn't even know if they were still together as friends, but in her heart, she hoped so... No, she *believed* so.

Alicia realized how much she had missed them while she had been back in her world. Being here again, in this realm, the memories of each came flooding back. Mickey the squirrel, with his sarcastic and untrusting ways, yet full of love and care for those he considered family. Briar's "CAW CAW" screechy voice, who had shown bravery for his small size. Fiona, the enigmatic deer who communicated not through words, but with thoughts and images that Alicia could see in her mind. They were drawn to each other by their shared losses and by Alicia's kind acceptance of their differences. She would never forget the loyalty and bonds they built with one another.

"I miss you guys," Alicia spoke to the wind, hoping her words would somehow, magically, carry to their ears. "I don't know what I would have done without you. I wish you were here now. I could really use your company." She glanced around the woods. "A cougar visited me in camp last night, with its tawny yellow eyes staring at me!" She shuddered. "I could use *your* eyes right now, Briar. You could definitely see from high up if that cat was coming back." She reached up and touched her shoulder where the squirrel had ridden for most of their journey. "And Mickey. Your voice in my ear was a constant reminder that I was not alone. I feel alone now."

Alicia felt a single tear form in the corner of one eye. She squinched her eyes shut and felt the tear start to run down her cheek, wiping it away quickly. She wasn't a child anymore. She had been a teenager for almost two years now! She had gotten through her first night on the other side, encountered a dangerous animal and survived. She was smart and strong; there was no doubt about that after last night! This journey would only take a couple of days at the most, and she'd be back with her family. She could do this.

Silently, she continued her journey towards Thunderbolt.

CH. 7 PATHS TAKEN

By mid-afternoon, Alicia reached the base of the mountain. Peering toward the top, she could see clouds gathering there, grayish but not dark, and she hoped they didn't signify the coming of rain.

Alicia thought of the lookout tower that sat so high in her world, where rangers could keep an eye out for forest fires usually started by lightning strikes. She hiked the mountain once before a couple of years earlier with her parents. They had driven to the trailhead and from there it took a couple hours to reach the top. The trail had been fairly easy for the most part, and she remembered a deep canyon they needed to traverse.

A bridge, made from metal cables and wood, crossed the gap and was fastened on either end to posts drilled into the rock of the canyon walls. Looking over the edge, she remembered seeing nothing but treetops, but she could hear the rushing river far below. The bridge was wide enough that two people could easily walk side by side, and she had held her father's hand while crossing, scared to look down but unable to resist. It was one of the most thrilling moments of her life!

They had stayed and visited with the ranger for an hour or so. Alicia was fascinated to learn more about what to watch for during the thunderstorms. The ranger explained how to identify a real fire threat from a simple campfire based on the color and thickness of the smoke. It only furthered her desire to become a ranger when she grew up, if the botanist thing didn't work out.

Eventually they said their goodbyes and left the lookout. Coming down the mountain had been much easier and faster, and they had gotten back to the cabin before nightfall. She didn't imagine the building would be there in this world, but she sure would have loved another mug of that hot chocolate.

Alicia started up the mountain, following the trail she had been on all afternoon. The path wandered back and forth in a pattern called switchbacks making the ascent less steep than going straight uphill, but her progress was significantly slower compared to when she had been on level ground. Alicia reluctantly accepted the fact that at this rate, she knew she would have to spend one more night camping before reaching the top. She silently prayed that the darkening clouds she had seen earlier would hold their contents longer. She did not want to deal with seeking cover from a storm.

What would she find when she got to the top? Would there be this primeval thing sitting on the peak, watching the world with bored eyes? She had no idea what it would look like! Mickey had never described any of the Ancients to her. He had only said that they were tired and weak from using their combined magic to seal away the Wild Side from the human realm.

Humans had destroyed the mountains and the forest with their aggressive mining and tree cutting, so Mickey had said. The Ancient Ones had watched their natural beauty slowly being wiped out. Normally averse to spending time in one another's company, the beings recognized the great threat that humans posed. And so they gathered together in a large southeastern valley. Together, they had used their magics to build a wall, an invisible barrier dividing the two worlds to shut out humankind for good, banishing them from the world of magic. The trio of Ancients drained their energies to do so. And into this void of power—left behind in the magic realm—was born the great yellow pine, Gran'Tree.

The massive tree was not exactly malevolent. He simply didn't give much consideration to the other creatures of the land. And why should he, did they show him consideration? He loomed as the biggest, grandest thing in the land, and they were small and weak. Like any schoolyard bully, he decided his size gave him the right to do as he pleased. And so he extended his roots far and wide, sucking up all the water in the land, the very life-blood of the realm. It caused The Drying, the great disaster that drove away many of the creatures of the lake, almost destroyed the realm, and ultimately killed her friend Bristleback, the fearsome but misunderstood mountain troll.

Alicia befriended that huge troll the same way she had befriended the other animals that made up her group of companions. The troll had known he was dying from the lack of water, but he kept it a secret from the group, preferring instead to enjoy spending his last moments with these new friends he called "family." In the end, even with the support of all her companions, Bristleback had ultimately given her the courage to face Gran'Tree.

And now, here she was back in this realm—The Wild Side—a place she never thought to return to, and sometimes she wondered if it had really existed at all. But it *did* exist, and she was here and her parents were in danger. Turning toward the cloudy mountain top, she wondered again what she would find there. And if it could help.

Early in the evening, Alicia heard the faint echo of moving water. Looking ahead, she spied the narrow canyon she had crossed with her father and remembered the rushing river deep in its base. Approaching the canyon now, she looked for the bridge once again, but saw no sign of it. She felt momentarily confused, as the teenager was almost positive she was close to the same spot that she and her parents had hiked up to the lookout station.

"Of course!" she exclaimed aloud, briefly silencing the insect noise that was building in volume as the air cooled around her. "The bridge was in *my* world. It wouldn't be here. But how do I cross?"

Alicia walked to the edge of the canyon and knelt down to carefully peer over into the abyss. A small wave of dizziness hit her as she stared at pointy tree-tops rising from below. It was a strange sensation to look down at the tops of trees. This must feel a bit like what it is to be a bird, though birds would not experience the same vertigo she felt at the moment. She imagined Briar sailing above the trees. What a wonderful view that must be!

She could not find a way to climb down to the bottom of the canyon. The stone walls were too sheer and even if there were handholds, she wasn't sure that she would have the courage to attempt it. Continuing to look over the ledge she saw that to her left, an enormous pine tree had fallen, spanning the gap and creating a bridge of sorts. Would it be strong enough to let her cross?

Alicia stood, brushed the dirt from her knees, walked over to where she had seen the tree and knelt once more to look over the edge. The tree lay wedged into the side of the cliff only a couple of feet below. It spanned the width of the canyon, with the crown and its branches resting on the far side. The tree was wide, maybe three feet across, though not as wide as the bridge had been in her world. Still, she had walked across narrower rocks and logs with no problem. *Yeah, but those hadn't been hundreds of feet in the air!* She thought with concern. *If I had fallen off those, the worst thing to happen would be getting my shoes wet in a stream.* Here the danger was much, *much* greater. And just the thought of that made her knees tremble.

Alicia scanned the canyon again, left and right. She could not see another clear route across the gap. She could continue walking along the edge and hopefully find a path down. But how long would that take? The sun had dropped behind the tree line at this point. The air was cooling and she knew nighttime was only a couple of hours away. And there was still the chance of rain. The grey clouds remained above her head, looking darker than before. There was no chance she could find a way down and back up the other side before nightfall. She didn't want to wait until tomorrow, potentially adding a full extra day to her trip. Worry for her parents filled her head.

No, she could do this. She *had* to do this. There was no other way.

Alicia changed position and sat down on the edge of the cliff. Sliding her walking stick between the straps of her backpack alongside the spear, she braced her hands in the dirt and stretched her legs over the ledge, feeling for the fallen tree below. The tip of her shoes touched the hard surface and, using her arms, she slowly lowered herself down, her backpack scraping behind her against the canyon wall. Standing once again on firm ground—*firm log*, she thought—Alicia was thankful for the recent growth spurt she had gone through which allowed her to reach the tree with her legs. Otherwise, she would have had to make a small jump, and that would have been heart-stopping.

She flexed her knees, bouncing up and down testing the strength and sturdiness of the tree to know it could bear her full weight. If it had moved or cracked during her test, she still could have flung herself back onto the small shelf behind her and scramble up to safety. The tree remained firm and her fear lessened somewhat. *Okay, let's do this,* she thought. Looking across the tree, she thought it was funny—not funny *ha ha* but funny *strange*—how here, only a few feet lower than she had been on the edge of the cliff, the distance to the other side seemed so much farther.

She stepped forward onto the tree. The wide and only slightly rounded surface of the log did not throw off her balance too much. Alicia could hear the wind whistling through the treetops beneath her and, below that, a great crashing of water against rocks.

Now that she teetered over a gaping chasm, her mind decided that it would be the perfect time to go rogue and she began to imagine what it would be like to slip and fall. To watch the tree slip away in slow motion as her hands uselessly attempted to clutch at the nothing. How long would it take to reach the bottom, unseen from here? Would her body smash through tree branches, spinning wildly like a pinwheel in the wind? She doubted she had the strength to grab one of those branches and stop her rapid descent. Maybe she would hit her head, knocking herself unconscious and fall limply toward her death. She hoped it was this last option. She didn't want to think about seeing the ground rush up to meet her as she dropped like a stone through the trees, watching the inevitable approach of the Grim Reaper standing there patiently waiting with his scythe on the jagged stones below.

Shaking off this awful thought, Alicia eased out slowly, making sure to plant each foot firmly before stepping forward with the next. The bark of the tree remained wet from the rain a couple evenings ago and she could feel her shoes slip the smallest amount with each step forward. An occasional gust of wind rose from below, catching her hair in its crisp, pine-scented fingers and swirling it in front of her eyes. In these moments she paused, waiting for the wind to die down, before brushing her hair away and moving forward again.

With every step she kept her eyes focused on the patch of tree in front of her, not daring to look over the edge. She didn't look up, didn't know how far she still had to go. *Concentrate. You can do this*, she thought. One step. Then one more. Then one more.

Suddenly she felt something other than the wind brush against her arm. Startled, Alicia looked up. At the same moment, her right shoe came down on a small patch of moss, soggy and slippery. Before she had time to register what was happening, her foot shot sideways into the open air and she felt herself falling.

Alicia flailed her arms wildly, trying to regain her balance, but with no success. Falling to one knee, she felt pain as her body began sliding over the edge of the tree. Suddenly, her arm hit something and she quickly hooked it around the object. Looking to her left at what she was holding, Alicia saw a branch sticking out from the side of the tree and that had curled up and around into the air. This is what had scraped her shoulder and startled her, she thought. Now her arm hooked around it and the branch appeared to bend precariously in her direction. Her fall momentarily halted, she glanced forward and noticed several more branches immediately ahead. And right past those was the other side!

Alicia pulled herself carefully back onto the tree, trying not to exert any extra force on the already stressed branch. She got her right leg up onto the surface and rested, with head bowed, inhaling deeply to regain the breath that the near-death experience had stolen from her lungs.

As she stayed there on hands and knees, a small ant climbed up and over the tip of her pinkie finger. Watching the small creature, her curious mind couldn't help but envision herself and the enormity of the task she set herself upon. This world was bigger than her. She was the ant, crawling across this log and heading forward into the unknown. She hoped that she could remain as sure-footed as the insect had appeared to be.

Remaining on her knees, Alicia used the branches ahead as handholds, cautiously crawling forward until she was once again above solid land. She lowered herself off the side of the huge tree, landing on the ground and stepping far away from the edge. She made it. She was across and one very large step closer to her destination.

Alicia glanced back the way she had come. As frightening as it had been, she had crossed and took some strength from that fact. Crossing back should feel a bit less stressful because she now knew what to expect. She would just crawl the entire way next time, but she wasn't looking forward to it.

Standing there, still waiting to get her breath back, Alicia rubbed her knee which still stung from the fall, and looked around. She was struck once again by the beauty of these woods having been so intently focused on her quest, that stopping to see what was around her hadn't been a priority. But now she took a moment to appreciate the view. Her gaze lingered on the canyon and she imagined a river, eons ago, slowly carving its way through the side of the mountain to create this. She had heard about the Grand Canyon in her world, and had seen pictures, but she never visited. What an amazing thing it must be! The absolute strength of time and the elements never ceased to fill her with wonder, and she felt ever so grateful to have spent her summers here in these woods, learning so much.

Breathing normally again, Alicia searched for a trail on this side. She found one continuing just a few yards away. *Clearly, I was not the first creature or person in this realm to use this as a bridge,* she thought. Renewed with a sense of accomplishment, she stepped onto the trail and continued toward the mountain peak and the Ancient waiting there.

CH. 8 THUNDERBOLT

The sky grew dark as Alicia approached the last section of her hike. The final half mile or so of trail became quite steep and she did not want to attempt this part at night. Quickly, she set about searching for a clearing well suited to build another camp.

She found a decent spot with relatively flat ground and enough trees surrounding the area to provide some shelter from the wind that had picked up over the past few hours of the climb. She removed her equipment and went about the task of gathering stones and wood.

Alicia kept scanning the forest worriedly. The memory of those yellow eyes staring into hers had not left her, and to make things worse, she heard sounds of stealthy movement throughout the day but did not see any sight of the cougar. However, she felt reasonably comfortable that the beast stayed behind when she began to climb the mountain.

The sky continued to darken as she worked, and, once again, Alicia saw the mysterious floating lights she had seen the previous night, this time seeing faint colors in the lights—soft shades of very pale reds, blues, and greens, among others. She still had no idea what they could be, but despite being intrigued, she turned her attention away and continued preparing camp. She vowed to research the lights as soon as she got back home with access to her books. She had one in particular that told of all the wildland creatures and was sure she would find the answer to these curious lights there.

Alicia quickly assembled a fire, pulled the blanket from her pack, and settled down in front of the growing flames to soak up the heat, which at the moment only reached her extended hands. The wind blew, and each gust brought a chill from the approaching storm. Alicia was thankful she had decided to bring the blanket, and wrapped it around her slim shoulders.

She passed a stream along the way, its water crashed down the mountain like a freight train, and there was no way to see if any fish hid in the froth. She had been unable to do much more than fill her water bottle, meaning that she had to make do with more jerky and trail mix for dinner.

Digging into her backpack once again, to get to the food bags that had found their way to the bottom. She took out the beef jerky that remained, turned back toward the fire, and found herself staring directly into the eyes of the cougar standing on the other side of the flickering fire; its head held low—watching her, unblinking, the rising flames of the blaze dancing in its eyes.

Just as the previous night, the teenager froze in place, not daring to move. The great cat remained motionless as well, as the firelight played along its flank highlighting the short and dusty, yellow fur. Alicia realized with panic that this night, she had no fish to share.

They stayed that way, with eyes locked, unmoving as the seconds ticked slowly, endlessly by. Alicia was terrified, but for some odd reason, she did not feel threatened by the cat. Oh, she knew it could easily kill her quickly, and painfully if it chose to, but somehow she got the sense that it wouldn't.

She felt her muscles relax and reached slowly into the bag of jerky, fingers blindly searching for and finding one of the bigger pieces. Those large, bright eyes tracked the motion of her hand with interest. Alicia gently withdrew the chunk of dried meat and, with as little movement as possible, tossed it in the direction of the cougar. It landed in the dirt with a soft *thump*. The cougar's eyes quickly darted toward the meat and then back toward the girl, but it remained motionless. Alicia reached into the bag again, taking out a smaller piece of jerky raising it to her lips, biting into the tough meat, then chewing.

The cat watched her for a moment longer, then lowered its head toward the chunk of meat resting near a huge paw. It sniffed at the piece, then gave a huff, sending a small cloud of dust swirling away from the jerky. The cat took the meat between its teeth, turning its head back toward the girl as it briefly chewed and then swallowed the treat.

Alicia took this moment to study the cougar more closely. The cat looked lean, but not skinny or undernourished. It had fur that almost matched the color of its eyes, and she could see the play of strong muscles along its flank. This beast was powerful, of that she was sure. She decided the cat was female. To her all cats seemed feminine and a quick, somewhat embarrassed, glance underneath its backside proved her right. Alicia began to think of the cat as a "her" rather than an "it." The cat had two parallel lines carved through the fur on her neck, where hair no longer grew. Alicia wondered what happened, thinking back to her encounter with a group of foxes three years ago that had left a small, thin scar along the back of her leg.

"How did you get that scar, you with the tawny eyes?" she asked quietly, almost a whisper. The cougar continued to look at her. "I am sorry I don't have any fish tonight," she said.

Alicia reached back into her bag of jerky and tossed another fat piece toward the large cat. This time, the cougar caught the piece of meat out of the air, bringing a small smile to the girl's lips.

"You're not going to hurt me, are you?" she asked softly, hope in her voice. "That is all I can share tonight. I need to save the rest."

The cat remained still, silently looking at her. After another moment, the cougar slowly blinked her golden eyes, turned away from the campfire and the girl, disappearing into the darkness.

"Goodbye, Tawny," Alicia whispered into the night. The only reply was the returning music of crickets.

Alicia had less difficulty falling asleep that evening. She felt slightly safer after this latest encounter with the powerful cat, feeling sure the cougar meant her no harm. She didn't know exactly why she thought that and wondered if she must be crazy for thinking so. She didn't plan on snuggling up to the cougar in the night anytime soon but did feel reasonably confident that the large cat was not going to kill her while she slept. The way the cat blinked those huge yellow eyes at her before leaving reassured her. Alicia had seen house cats do that when they felt comfortable around a person. Was it any different here? Other than this cat having three-inch-long "murder talons?" She didn't think so.

With this thought spinning through her head, Alicia laid down, wrapped the blanket more tightly around herself, and drifted off to sleep. Strange dreams of falling through a cloud of glowing lights and calling for Fiona to stop her descent wracked her sleep. She landed softly in a huge field of flowers and felt a malevolent presence nearby. The large cat suddenly appeared from nowhere to stand over her. Saliva dripped from its bared teeth, landing cold on her cheek.

The dream startled Alicia awake, and she found that first light had come. With it so had the rain, spattering lightly on her face. Alicia quickly broke camp, and, even though the rain had started, still went through the ritual of ensuring the fire was completely extinguished. Her parents ingrained fire safety rules in her since she was young enough to understand, there was so much life to be lost in a forest fire: trees, flowers, grasses, animals, even people and pets, too. She took the task seriously.

Sure that the fire was dead, Alicia popped some trail mix into her mouth, crunching on the variety of nuts and dried fruit. She put the bag of food away and shouldered her backpack, once again stowing her spear under the straps. She looked up the trail, remembering that this had been the most difficult part of the hike when she came with her parents. Sighing heavily and pushing wet hair from her eyes, she set off up the mountain—the final stretch of this journey.

The climb was as bad as she remembered, worse because of the rain, and with a quarter of a mile left, it got so steep it was almost vertical! She fell into a rhythm—*step, step, step, paauusse. Step, step, step, paauusse*—over and over, her leg muscles burning from the exertion. She used the walking stick for leverage to help pull her up every few feet. She could see the top now, surrounded by dark thunderclouds. She was almost there!

Approaching the peak, Alicia could make out the roof of a cabin or hut through the driving rain that had become a serious downpour. The rumble of thunder filled the sky and carried across the lake valley below. The sound had not quite faded when another louder boom, cracked above her chasing the first.

As she slowly crested the rise, more of the cabin came into view. Alicia squinted her eyes and peered at it. The shack was small and disheveled and the roof sagged into the rest of the building. It looked like nobody had lived here for a very long time.

Suddenly, a tremendous flash of light speared down from the black clouds, striking the cabin's metal chimney. Sparks flew everywhere, and the concussive force almost knocked the young girl off her feet.

Alicia scampered behind a tree and shouted toward the collapsing building. "Hellooo!" she yelled out, hearing nothing. "Helloooooo!!!" There was only silence in return and the steady beat of the rain.

She stepped cautiously from behind the tree and stood on the peak with her hands on her hips, looking across the vast landscape. Even through the falling rain, she could see to the opposite end of the lake sprawled below her ringed by soft, rounded mountains. If she looked carefully, she could almost see exactly where her cabin would be in her world, right on that small point that stuck out from the shore on the far side.

Cupping her hands around her mouth, Alicia screamed at the top of her lungs. "HELLOOOOOO!!!" The sounds carried out through the storm, and she could hear it echoing around the valleys below. However, only silence came from the small hut behind her.

She sat on a large boulder, letting the backpack and spear fall to the soaked ground, and stared out into the empty space before her. Her shoulders slumped, and her hair hung down around her face in long wet strands. What was she to do now? The Ancient One wasn't here and she had been counting on its help! Sure, there were two more beings out there—Vulcan and the Silver King—but if Thunderbolt wasn't here, why should she believe the others were still around?

Alicia felt lost. The great responsibility of what she was trying to accomplish came crashing down on her. Her parents were trapped, and she didn't know if there was any way to save them. She had convinced herself that she would find answers here atop this mountain. It was almost as if she had been called. And—hadn't she? Alicia thought back to several nights ago in the cabin when she awakened from a dream with a voice lingering in her head. "Cooome... fiiinnd meee." That's what it had said, right? The memory was foggy now, but she was sure it had been something like that. Well, here she was! She had come to find... who?

Alicia looked back toward the small cabin. Maybe there were answers within. Maybe she could find some clue as to where the Ancient One had gone. Standing up, she brushed off the back of her wet jeans and walked toward the house, watching the dark sky carefully. The door was barely attached with rusty hinges and had an old, beaten door handle. It didn't look safe to enter, but she had to try something.

Suddenly the small door of the cabin burst open and out strode a man of tremendous height. "Who is doing all the yelling out here and disturbing my sleep?" he boomed. "Oh," he said with a small start of surprise. "It's you!"

Alicia was taken aback by the banging of the door, but now she looked at the man. He was tall, at least six and a half feet, maybe even seven. He stood there dressed in what looked like old bedclothes, as disheveled as the cabin he called home. His hair was long and grey, hanging just below his shoulders. He had a thick mustache, but no beard. He had bare legs and wore no shoes. The man sort of looked like a cowboy from the old west, but without the horse, boots, and spurs. Strangest of all was that he seemed to recognize her.

"You know who I am?" Alicia asked, curiously.

"Well, of course I do, Alicia. I've known you for a very long time." The man stepped forward, his bedclothes flapping behind him, and approached the girl. "You saved this realm. You did what you were born to do. And now you're back. Why are you back? Your role is done. It ended long ago."

Alicia was confused by this barrage of statements, trying to sort them out in her head as the man spoke quickly. "Wait, wait, wait. How have you known me for a very long time? And how did you know I saved this realm? And how could my role have ended long ago, when I was only here three years ago?" She paused her questioning for a moment to take a breath before continuing. "And I need to know. Are you the Ancient known as Thunderbolt?"

"All good questions, and all with good answers, sure. But, one at a time," he chided her. He placed his arm on her shoulder, leading her back toward the boulder where she had been resting. Gently guiding her to a sitting position and settled himself to the ground, his head now level with hers. The man raised his face to the sky and waved his hand. The rain stopped immediately, as if turning off a kitchen faucet, and the dark clouds slowly dissipated into the atmosphere.

Lowering his head to look the girl in the face, he smiled and said, "My word, you really have grown. But you're still quite young. There is so much potential."

He paused, continuing to look at her. Alicia squirmed under his scrutiny.

"Yes, child, I am Thunderbolt."

CH. 9 CONFESSION

Alicia breathed a huge sigh of relief. She'd done it! She found Thunderbolt. All of the questions and fears that swirled around her mind over the past few days all tumbled out in a rush.

"Oh my goodness, Mr. Thunderbolt, sir. I came here looking for you! My family, my parents are... stuck in this... I don't know... Some sort of weird invisible bubble. They are frozen, not moving." The words came flowing from her mouth like water.

"I tried to save them, I tried. I smashed the bubble with the biggest rock I could hold, over and over until my hands bled. But nothing happened!"

She paused for a moment. A small sob escaped her throat like the low bark of a dog. "But it's not just them. There are bubbles everywhere! I don't know how many and I don't know why. My only thought was that maybe I could find an answer here. Find a way to save them." Alicia looked at the Ancient One in front of her. "My hope was that *you* could save them," she finished, looking deflated after the rush of words.

Thunderbolt looked at the girl, his eyes filled with sadness. "Oh child, I have no real magic left, and the little I have is just enough to keep me alive year after year."

"But I just saw you do magic!" she insisted. "I saw the rain and clouds disappear."

The Ancient waved his hand dismissively. "Tricks, nothing more. Simple spells and illusions to keep others away and protect my solitude." He raised his head toward the lake and beyond to the south, his gray eyes looking weary. "Our magic was depleted. Most of what I regained, I gave to you centuries ago."

"Gave to me?" Alicia asked, confused. "You gave nothing to me. We have never met."

"You are correct, child. We have never met," he said, continuing to stare into the distance. "But still,

I gave you my magic. Can't you feel it? I sense it in you. It called you here long ago."

"You called me here?" she asked, confused by these answers.

"Yes," he replied. "Only you had the power to stop Gran'Tree. You were needed, and you came. You did exactly what we expected. You defeated the greatest threat this realm has faced." Thunderbolt looked back at Alicia. "But that was the last of it. The last of my true magic. I have waited here for *centuries*, waiting for it to come back to me. But there's nothing. It's in you now. It is a part of you. *My* magic is *yours*."

"But how could you have waited for centuries?" she asked. "You only called me here three years ago."

"Alicia," he said looking into her eyes, "over four thousand years have passed since you last set foot in these lands."

Alicia stared at the Ancient in shock, her mouth agape. She couldn't think straight, her mind all jumbled. Trying to process by this information after a minute or two, she blurted out, "What do you mean, four thousand years? It's only been three! I was eleven the last time I was here."

"Ahhh, but you see, child, time works differently between the two realms, as you should very well know. Answer me this. How long did you stay in the Wild Side when you were last here?"

Alicia thought back, trying hard to remember. "I don't know exactly, it was so long ago. But several nights passed. It might have been as long as two weeks."

"And when you returned, how much time had passed in your world?"

She thought hard. She remembered facing Gran'Tree, the rain pouring down around her. She turned away from the great tree and saw her dad there, kneeling in the grass and the dirt. Had he waited there for the whole two weeks? No, that didn't make sense. Wait, that's right! He thought that she was gone only a little while, that she was playing some sort of hide-and-seek game. And when she tried to explain what happened, her father had brushed it off like it was a make-believe fantasy, scolding her for hiding when they were trying to beat the storm home.

Realization slowly dawned on Alicia. The Ancient was right! Time *did* work differently here. What had only been a moment for her father in her world had been days, maybe weeks, for her in the Wild Side. And now she was three years older. Had four thousand years really passed here in *this* realm? She could hardly believe it. No wonder everything looked so overgrown and different when she crossed the barrier. But that meant...

She thought of her friends, Mickey, Fiona, and Briar. Now she understood why she had not seen them. They would all be dead now, wouldn't they? Gone to dust many generations ago. The thought saddened her, but she knew that was the way of things. She believed they had remained friends throughout their lives. Different and unique, yes, definitely argumentative at times, but still friends. She knew in her heart it was true. At least she understood why they were not there to greet her, and she didn't feel quite so abandoned.

With the realization came a sudden idea. "Do you think that is why my parents are trapped? Do you think that maybe the differences in the way time works caused this? Maybe, somehow, your time has... leaked across the barrier into my world, creating those time bubbles or whatever they are."

"You could be right, child," Thunderbolt agreed. "Maybe Gran'Tree's great roots pushed against that barrier, weakening it over the years. After you faced him, he withered from the loss of water. His roots grew smaller as well. Perhaps when they withdrew, they left behind gaps in the barrier," he mused. "Today, the tree is a shriveled husk of his former self, alone there in that meadow where it all started."

"What do you mean, 'where it started?'" Alicia questioned. "Where *what* started?"

Thunderbolt heaved a great sigh. "I guess it's time this story was told. Some of it you may already know. But not all of it. Not our worst sin. So listen, child. Listen and remember."

A massive meadow blanketed the wide-open space filled with grasses and wildflowers of all colors. A gentle summer breeze flowed through the valley, carrying across the meadow all the great varieties of scents from the many blossoms. In this field no trees had ever grown, for the roots of the flowers choked the life from any new sapling that tried to sprout. A more beautiful location could not have been chosen.

It was there, this untouched place, that three beings met. They came together to privately discuss the threat of humankind. Individually, their magic was strong—the charge of lightning held by Thunderbolt, the blazing heat belonged to Vulcan, and the very power of the earth possessed by the Silver King. Combined, their powers could alter the very fabric of time and space.

They agreed that they must do something if the world was to survive. So they worked great magics, combining earth and fire and lightning, understanding that doing so would weaken them immensely. Strained and sweating, each of the Ancients reached deep inside themselves, amassing a strength not seen since the creation of the world.

The power of their combined strength tore apart the very sky itself. A ripping sound filled the air, echoing across mountains and through canyons, like rending the largest bed sheet in the world right down the middle. Even though it was early afternoon, stars appeared briefly in the heavens above their group before walls of daylight came crashing back together and clouds filled the sky. Powerful shock waves radiated from a single point where the trio gathered, vibrating every living thing like a plucked piano string. Rain poured down, dousing them using a deluge of cold water, as if God himself desired to wash away this offending abuse of power.

When the vibrations stopped and the thunder faded away, a heavy silence descended on the land. As the rain continued to fall, they looked at one another, tired and slumped from the effort. Thunderbolt, Vulcan, and the Silver King knew they had severed the world of magic from the world of humans, never to mix again. They had succeeded. "Let humankind destroy their own world," they said. In time, this realm would heal.

Without another word to each other, they turned and left, returning to their own domains to rest and recover.

"We left the meadow that day never knowing what a terrible being our forces had created." Thunderbolt paused, remembering back. "You see, borne on those beautiful summer winds that smelled so gloriously of flowers," he continued, "had been a tiny seed never seen by any of us, though truly even if we had looked, we would have paid it no attention. After all, seeds are common in these wooded lands. What was one more? But this seed, you see, was special! This seed landed just so, right in the center of our group as we talked and debated, and the winds danced around us." The once majestic Thunderbolt looked terribly sad, his bedclothes hanging loosely on his frame. "And when we finally wrought the powerful magics between us, it was right on the spot where that seed lay. That very seed absorbed a great deal of that magic."

Alicia listened, knowing what was coming next, but not wanting to hear it. "That seed, that unassuming *little seed*, sprung from a simple looking pine cone from a non-descript tree not so far away. The magic, *our* magic, gave this seed strength. It drank so deeply from the rain that poured down. Water—the additional missing element to our own of sky, fire, and earth—sped the growth in ways we could not have known and could never have imagined! Its roots were bigger and stronger than the flowers that normally sucked all the nutrients from the ground."

Thunderbolt breathed deeply, gathering the courage to continue. "And so, in our desire to rid this realm of humankind, we created a monster even more terrible. Uncaring. Unknowing. Just existing. Surviving at all costs. We created Gran'Tree."

Alicia closed her eyes and bowed her head, the weight of this revelation was sinking in. She recalled the previous Halloween when she had watched an old black and white movie with her father called *Frankenstein*. It was about a doctor trying to bring the dead back to life, trying to control a power that was reserved only for God. The monster he created was childlike, not understanding why he existed. In the end, the villagers, fearing what they did not know, killed the monster. Alicia remembered crying and feeling sympathy for the creature who never had the choice to live again and was now condemned to die.

She thought of the great tree. Unlike Frankenstein's monster, *his* understanding had grown over the ages so that by the time she met and spoke with him, he knew what he was doing and just didn't care. She felt no sympathy for him. He deserved to be destroyed.

She looked back up into the storm grey eyes of Thunderbolt. "You believed yourselves gods" she said quietly, with an almost scolding tone in her voice. "You tried to shape the world to your own vision, and in the process almost lost everything. You may have had power, but you were no gods."

The man looked exhausted from the telling. "You are right. We stepped beyond our bounds and these lands paid the price. If we had only waited a moment longer, perhaps we would have seen the seedling sprout and grow so unnaturally," he said with regret. "But I believe we were all ashamed in some way of what we had done. Standing there, looking at each other, we saw that shame reflected in each other's eyes. So we left without speaking. Never spoke again, until..." Thunderbolt paused in the telling.

"Until what?" Alicia questioned.

"Oh child, there is so much you don't know yet. We tried to make it right. At least some of us did. You have magic within you. So much potential," he said, repeating the words from earlier. Thunderbolt looked at the girl a moment longer, then stood and turned away, walking slowly back to the dilapidated hut.

"Where are you going?" Alicia called out to him. "I need your help!"

"You came to the wrong place, child," he said, not turning around. "I have no more help to give, child, and no more desire to talk." The shame of his story had slumped his frame to the point where he appeared almost a foot shorter than when she first saw him.

"But I need you! What about my parents?!" she yelled at his back, anger and frustration pouring out through her words. "And I have so many questions!"

The being paused. Turning back toward her he said, "Go see Vulcan. My story is done, and I no longer have the strength or energy to help you with this matter. I have given you protection. I can give you nothing more. Go to Vulcan. Maybe there you will find the answers you seek."

With that, the great Ancient of thunder turned away. Pulling open the rickety door of the cabin, he went inside. Her last image of him was that of a gnarled hand reaching back to pull the door shut, and then Thunderbolt was gone.

CH. 10 GOING HOME

Alicia banged on the door of the small cabin and hollered for Thunderbolt to answer, but only silence greeted her. She tried to turn the handle, but it was locked from the inside. "Unbelievable!" she spat. Frustrated and tired, she gave up and turned away.

She stepped to the edge of the mountain top and looked to the southwest, far beyond where her cabin would have been, just past the large clearing known in her world as Stolle Meadows. Not the same meadow that Gran'Tree had once presided over, but still a sizeable place. She knew hot springs dotted the hills beyond where she would find the next Ancient, Vulcan.

It was only lunchtime, and she still had most of the day ahead of her. Alicia walked to the door and banged on it one last time before turning toward the trail, starting to make her way back down the mountain. The girl felt disappointed beyond belief because she had hoped that Thunderbolt would have the solution. Instead, she left his domain filled with new questions that had no answers.

What did he mean 'I gave you my power'? she thought. He said he could see it in me. Others have said so, too. But, if it's true, why can't I use it?

Frustration upon frustration built up inside of her. Alicia hadn't discovered a solution to save her parents, there was magic in her that she could not use, and all she had found was a tired old man who refused to help her. And now, she had to travel over twice as far as she had to the top of Thunderbolt's mountain, all for the small hope, *the tiny chance,* that the Ancient called Vulcan would have the answers she needed.

"AARRGGGHHH!" she screamed standing alone above the treetops, balling her fists and letting pent up frustration out into the world. She stamped her feet on the ground and raised her face to the sky. "AARRGGGHHH!!!"

She screamed until she was out of breath, then stood there, letting the frustrated, negative energy drain from her limbs. Her mind went over everything she knew, trying to assemble the facts as she saw them, thinking analytically about the situation like she did when preparing for a test at school.

Ok, so I was called to the Wild Side, and Thunderbolt gave me his magic to defeat Gran'Tree. Was that the 'protection' he said he'd given me? Why couldn't he defeat the tree himself? And why did he say I was born to do this? Again, more questions with no answers, but she had learned something. She learned the origin of the terrible yellow pine. And she learned that even beings with tremendous strength are fallible. One should never play lightly at being God. One should never play God at all.

"All right, fine!" she said, spinning around and yelling up toward the mountain's peak. "I'll go talk to Vulcan. Do I have any other choice?" She didn't think Thunderbolt would hear her, and even if he did, he had made it clear that he was finished talking.

Alicia resolved to continue on to the next Ancient and made her way down the mountain, collecting berries and chewing on handfuls of trail mix along the way. At least the rain had stopped. She reached the narrow canyon with the fallen tree. Crossing back was scary, but this time she crawled the whole way across.

Alicia considered the time differences again—*four thousand years, was it really possible?* Of course, she knew that it was. It all made sense. If fifteen minutes of her world's time equaled two weeks here, then three years must equal... the truth is, she didn't want to do the math. She'd already done enough homework this summer, but she certainly believed it could be over four thousand years.

Back at home and in school, she had rarely thought about her friends from the Wild Side, but now, as she walked down the mountain trail, she took a moment to mourn them. They had been an interesting bunch, and they supported her in this strange place during her last visit. Were they drawn to her by her magic? Was that the core that brought them all together? She knew that the feeling of being a strange little family held them together throughout their short journey, but had magic been that initial connection, unknown but felt in a way they couldn't explain? Maybe. And maybe, that same magic drew the great cat to her!

Thinking about the cougar, Alicia quickly searched the woods but saw no sign of the beast. That did not mean much, though. She hadn't seen the cat at all the previous day. It moved like some kind of ninja cat, always blending into the surroundings. Tawny, Alicia's name for the golden-eyed cat, had certainly shown up when night fell, looking for food and she fully expected to see her again tonight.

Those huge yellow eyes were magnificent and hypnotizing. *Yes, Tawny,* she thought. It was a good name, fitting for the cougar.

Alicia continued to pick her way down the mountainside following the trail for the most part, at one point veering toward a river she heard in the distance. Hoping to find the waterway wide and rapid enough to spot some fish, the young adventurer was in luck. The river here was not as rough as she had seen earlier, with deeper pools downstream behind a few large boulders. Eddies formed there, small pockets where the water would get caught and spin endlessly like a miniature whirlpool. These were perfect spots to find fish, and she ended up spearing two—one for her and one for Tawny—just in case. She wrapped the fish tightly in the huge leaves of nearby skunk cabbage and placed them into her pack, positioning them so that they would stay wrapped, keeping the raw fish from touching her other things.

Alicia reached the bottom of the mountain before dark and had plenty of time to set up camp for the night. She was becoming quite the pro at this and had a fire going in record time. As she worked, she saw the floating lights were back. By this time, it would have felt strange for them *not* to show up, and her curiosity about them grew. *Are they trying to lure me away, to get me to follow them?* The idea frightened her. Clearly, she still had undiscovered magic to learn about in this realm.

Her first fish was cooked perfectly, and while she worked on the second, as expected, Tawny walked slowly into the firelight. Alicia felt a shiver travel up her spine, but no longer felt the terror of before. Once again, she extended the stick with the semi-cooked fish on it toward the cat. Tawny did not lunge this time, but instead stretched her neck forward and grasped the fish in her jaws. Pulling away, she sat back on her haunches and slowly chewed the fish, swallowing until it was gone. Alicia didn't know if the cat preferred the fish cooked, but she sure didn't seem to mind it that way.

After finishing her meal, Tawny watched the girl for a few seconds longer. *Did she want something else*, Alicia wondered? The answer was no. After staring a minute more, the great cat once again turned and faded into the night. Alicia wondered where she went. *Was she off hunting for more food? Was she staying nearby, but just out of sight?* Alicia didn't know, but she no longer worried about it. The cat was just another companion of sorts. One that didn't stay around and nor did it talk to her. It remained present nevertheless. In a small way, Alicia took comfort in that knowledge.

The following day was mostly uneventful; she passed the time counting deer off in the distance and found frogs in a small pond. Watching them hop away as she approached reminded her of being younger and all the exploring she used to do. Alicia had left some of that behind in the past year or so, as she delved further into reading, studies, and hanging out with friends.

She absolutely loved losing herself in a good book, and fantasy was her favorite, especially *A Wrinkle in Time*. She had read through *The Lord of the Rings* series and finished *The Chronicles of Narnia* recently, which in some ways reminded her of her time at the lake and the amazing adventures she always experienced. Lately, she'd been reading more science fiction stories, which she loved almost as much as fantasy.

Even though she didn't explore as much as she used to, Alicia still thoroughly enjoyed being outdoors, and she had places around the lake that were considered extra magical. Within days—sometimes within hours—of arriving for any visit to the cabin, Alicia would always make a point to visit those special places. She thought of them as *her* places, and sometimes she needed only to touch base and restore the harmonic rhythms within her soul.

Alicia wondered how many of those places existed here in this realm and would love to go looking for them, but she didn't have the time. However, the thought sparked an idea. She decided to make a small detour which required briefly leaving the path she was on, but it shouldn't impact her travel too much. After all, if time flowed differently here, then only moments would pass in her world. She was curious to see the location of her cabin in this realm and compare differences if any existed.

It was late afternoon when she reached a spot on the trail that she felt was close to where the road turnoff leading to her cabin should be, though things looked very out of place. Like one of those "spot the difference" puzzles where you compare two similar, but not quite identical pictures, her mental picture of here was one thing, but the reality of this realm had striking variations. She saw a huge tree here, or one missing there, and bushy plants that didn't belong.

Hiking off-trail again was a chore, but thoughts of what she might find kept the girl's motivation high. Beginning to sweat in the afternoon heat, she stuffed her light jacket into her backpack, and the small number of scratches she collected on her bare arms didn't deter her. Alicia thrashed quickly through bushes and stepped lively over the fallen trees that occasionally barred her path. When the passage was clear, she enthusiastically picked up speed even more, planning to camp on the very spot where her bed rested in her world. Wouldn't that be unique!

After another hour or so of hiking, she could make out the familiar shape of the lake shore in the distance, and she increased her pace. Moving quickly now, she reached the point where her cabin would have been, dropping her gear to the ground.

Alicia closed her eyes and stood there, listening to the sounds of the forest and feeling the wind kiss away the sweat on her forehead, trying to sense her world and the energies there. She held her breath, waiting.

After a few moments, she slowly exhaled and opened her eyes. Nothing. She felt no connection to the once familiar spot. Alicia looked around. This area had little resemblance to her world. The trees were in different places, and the large boulder in front of her cabin was gone. *Well, of course*, she thought. *Centuries have passed here, eons! Everything would be different.* She walked to where she estimated her bed stood, finding a large tree growing right up through what would have been her pillow.

Suddenly, she had an idea and scanned the environment again, comparing it to her mental map. "Yes, right there." Stepping away from the tree, Alicia walked forward slowly, carefully searching the air in front of her, but there was still nothi...wait! *Oh my...*, she thought. Hanging in the air directly ahead was the thinnest sliver of light. Its color shining through a slightly different tone than the rest of the world. She would never have seen it if she hadn't been looking so intently for it.

Leaning forward, she pressed her eye close to the sliver of light and was able to look through! It was sort of like looking through a kaleidoscope where the other side is all jumbled and distorted, but there, right there where she last saw them in her world, were two figures she would recognize anywhere. "Mom and Dad," she whispered almost reverently, a small cry escaped her.

They stood frozen on the other side of the disturbed air, just like she had left them, trapped within their bubble of time. *So it was true*, she thought, tears rolling down her cheeks at the sight of them. *The barrier had cracked, and now it's leaking into our world.* She didn't know how much chaos this had caused.

"Gran'Tree!" she barked angrily, pulling away from the small crack. It wasn't enough that in his prime he had come close to destroying the Wild Side. Evidently he had weakened the barrier so much that now after his defeat, his actions threatened to destroy her world as well!

My actions, she suddenly thought. After all, she was the one who had defeated Gran'Tree. If she had never crossed over the barrier, if she had never faced the great tree, would all this have still happened? Great guilt descended on her. Yes, in some ways she was as much to blame as the grand tree was.

But she was called. Summoned. What had Thunderbolt said? She had done what she was born to do. He had called her, and she came. Did that mean that she had no free will? Was her destiny already planned out from birth?

No, she refused to accept that. Her decisions were her own. The Ancient Ones liked to think they were in control, liked to think they could play gods. But look where that had gotten them. Alicia seethed with anger. If there was anyone to blame here, it was them. Beings that thought themselves all-powerful and severed two worlds, but in the process unleashed a monster that might ultimately destroy *both* worlds! She felt furious at the thought of it.

The sun sank, and already, the forest grew darker than she realized. Alicia quickly set up camp near the pillow tree. She hadn't gotten a chance to fish that evening, caught up in the excitement of seeing the location of her cabin, so she settled for another meal of jerky and nuts.

Tawny did not come around that evening. Alicia waited, pieces of dried meat sitting by her side for the beast, but the cat never showed. Perhaps she felt Alicia's anger, or sensed it. Maybe she'd had enough of traveling with the human and chose to go her own way. Alicia sort of missed the cat. After three nightly visits, she started to grow fond of the cougar, even if the sojourns were brief.

She didn't see the small dancing lights this evening either. *Strange,* she thought. *Could their absence be connected to Tawny's?* She didn't see how but would have to think about it more, later when her head was clearer.

Settling down for the night, she pulled the blanket over herself while the heat from the fire warmed one side of her body. Alicia's thoughts grew heavy. She expected to arrive at her destination tomorrow, and her mind went to the upcoming meeting with Vulcan where she would demand answers. Her last thought before falling asleep was hope that the Ancient would be more forthcoming than Thunderbolt had been.

Alicia's eyes flicked open, her senses suddenly alert. She heard something. Something familiar and frightening that awakened the oldest and most primeval section of her brain, the one that controlled the fight or flight instinct.

She had been lost in a troubled dream, the details of which flitted away like butterflies, bits of color scattering on the breeze. But, a sound had awoken her, bringing her neatly and cleanly out of the dream and into full wakefulness.

Alicia lay there, listening intently, her eyes nervously scanning the forest. The hastily assembled fire had died down to nothing but glowing embers, providing very little light. But the moon, almost full now, shone through the tree branches above, creating bright spots among the pockets of darkness. Within one of these pockets, she saw a vaguely recognizable outline of something else. Something she was absolutely sure had not been there when she fell asleep.

"Tawny," Alicia called to the shape in the shadows. "Is that you?"

The thing in the shadows lifted its face to the moon—and howled.

CH. 11 A BOND FORMED

Alicia leapt to her feet and grabbed one of the last remaining sticks from the fire; one end glowed with a red-hot ember. She held the stick in front of her, pointing it at the grey wolf that now emerged from the shadows, its head low and teeth bared. The fur along its neck stuck up in a ridge that extended along the full length of its back.

She blindly reached down to the ground with her left hand, searching, her eyes focused on the wolf in front of her. Closing her fingers around the object she found there, Alicia stood back up to full height, carrying the makeshift spear in her left hand. Standing in the darkness, a weapon in each hand, she could have been mistaken for the primitive warrior she imagined herself as in the past. But she was no warrior, just a young girl scared out of her wits and ready to do anything necessary to survive.

Another howl rose from her left. *Of course,* she thought, panicked, *wolves hunt in packs.* She glanced to her left seeing nothing but darkness, so she returned her focus to the immediate threat—the wolf facing her, slowly circling the remains of the fire.

Alicia thrust the stick with the glowing ember forward, swinging it rapidly back and forth, the red-hot tip leaving traces of light in the night air.

"GET OUT OF HERE!" she shouted in desperation. "GO AWAY!"

The wolf backed off and she had a momentary feeling of relief, but the wolf only looked for another path to circle around the girl. Alicia cocked her arm back and threw the spear as hard as she could at the wolf, but she used her left hand and the aim was off. Instead of the perfectly straight line she'd imagined, the spear flip-flopped through the air, its side striking the wolf's flank. Not at all strong enough to wound the beast, but hard enough to hurt it, causing the wolf to duck into the darkness of the woods to her right.

She leaped forward quickly and scooped up the thrown spear, spinning back toward the fire just as the previously unseen wolf came charging from the darkness growling ferociously. Alicia swung the spear in its direction, the worn point facing outward, which brought the wolf to a stop, his snarling muzzle revealed fangs, white and shining in the moonlight. She waved the ember at him, but this animal refused to back away. It lowered its upper body close to the ground, a deadly growl coming from deep in its throat. She could smell the stench of death on its breath.

Alicia was terrified. She didn't know where the first wolf went. Perhaps it ran off for good when it was hit with the spear, but she doubted it. She wanted to search for it, but she dare not take her eyes from the beast in front of her which showed more courage than the one that fled.

Alicia watched the wolf's muscles flex and tense. She sensed him preparing to jump and started planning her next move when something large and golden raced past her on her left, knocking her onto her back and making her lose her grip on both weapons.

Tawny!

The cat leaped on top of the wolf in an instant, slashing with her sharp talons and ripping long bloody fissures into the side of the beast. Caught unaware by this attack, the wolf struggled to get back on its feet, clawing and snapping at the great cat but unable to connect.

Alicia watched from her position on the ground, lying on her back. She could see the wolf trying in vain to fight back against the larger, fiercer cougar. Suddenly she heard a soft growl behind her. Craning her neck to look over her shoulder, she saw the first wolf—the one that she hoped had fled—crawling forward very low to the ground, almost on its belly, sneaking in.

The animal stretched forward, grabbing her ponytail in its teeth. Intense pain blossomed across her scalp and her hands flew to her head as the wolf began to drag her away while the great cat was distracted. Defenseless and holding her hair, trying to prevent it from being ripped out, she screamed, "NOOOO!"

In a flash, Tawny loomed above her, paws on either side of Alicia's body. Alicia felt the immediate release of her hair looked up to see nothing but the underside of the cat's chin and the white fur that trailed down her belly. The cat screeched savagely at the retreating wolf, protecting the girl, shielding her with her enormous body. A drop of saliva, hot and wet, fell from the cougar's stretched lips, landing on the frightened girl's cheek.

Despite Alicia's growing trust in the creature above her, this was all too much. She rolled on her side, curled into a ball, closed her eyes, and prayed silently. If there was ever a time she needed saving, now was that time.

The wolf at Alicia's feet was gone, limping off somewhere to nurse its wounds, or perhaps even to die. The one that remained stared at the cat, face to face, for a long moment before turning tail and fleeing as well. Tawny snarled loudly after the beast before turning her face down and looking at the figure beneath her.

In the silence that ensued, Alicia opened her eyes and looked up into the face of the cat. She saw fury in those golden orbs which frightened her.

However, as she watched, the fury seemed to melt away, replaced by something else. The cat's features softened, while her big, furry chest heaved from the efforts of the fight. The cat looked at Alicia for a few seconds more then stepped gently away, leaving the girl exposed and dazed by the experience.

Alicia slowly sat up, examining the area around her. There were streaks of blood, black as shadows in the moonlight, where the two creatures had fought. She looked at Tawny and saw blood there too, but she didn't know if it had come from the cougar or the wolf.

The cat paced back and forth around the edge of the sleeping area Alicia had set up for herself. Clearly agitated, the cat made small huffing noises at whatever might still be lurking out in the darkness, occasionally letting loose a louder growl, a clear warning to anything that might consider returning.

Alicia crawled over to the stick with the burning ember and retrieved it. She searched the ground around it, making sure no stray sparks had ignited anything, then returned the stick to the fire. Gathering some small twigs from nearby, she piled them around the ember, along with some "witches' hair" moss she'd collected from the low-hanging branches of a tree. She blew gently on the ember, watching it grow brighter until a small flame took form and lit the rest of the material. Alicia added more small sticks to the flame and then sat down beside it, watching the orange colors dance, feeling her heart rate slow gradually. She didn't think she would get any more sleep tonight.

Tawny continued to pace for a few minutes more, then lowered herself to the ground on the opposite side of the fire. Alicia understood that something had changed between them. The great cat would not leave her side tonight.

Morning dawned and darkness left the forest, dragging with it the terror of the night before. Alicia stood slowly, stretching her leg muscles which had cramped from being in a sitting position all night. In the light of day, the red blood on the ground stood out, a stark contrast to the brown dirt and dead pine needles.

Tawny rose as well. There were no longer streaks of blood on her. Alicia imagined the cat must have spent the night cleaning itself, while she was lost in the depths of the flames, unaware of anything else all night.

The girl felt sore and tired this morning, a combination of tension and adrenaline from the attack. She wandered down to the lakeshore where the reeds along the shore had grown tall and wild. Pushing through, Alicia dipped her hands into the cold water. She scooped up some of the lake water, splashing it on her face and head, trying to shock some life back into herself. One splash was not enough, so she dipped into the water a few more times, then scooped handfuls of water and used them to wash her bare arms, cleaning off several days of sweat and dirt, wincing as she rinsed and cleaned the small scratches. Once satisfied, she returned to her campsite, water dripping from her wet hair onto her shoulders.

As she walked, feeling somewhat refreshed, her mind wandered. *Did she save me because I gave her a few bits of fish and jerky? That can't be! Is she part of the magic that Thunderbolt gave me—not her, but the connection between Tawny and me? This makes no sense, but neither does anything else!*

Tawny had disappeared from the campsite. Alicia looked around and spotted the great cat a few yards away moving through the brush, no longer hiding her presence from the girl. Alicia smiled at this realization, happy to know they had formed an unusual bond. She didn't quite know what it meant yet, but she felt certain now that the cat would never harm her and might even take care of her.

She gathered her things and put out the fire, took food from the pack, and saw that her rations were about half gone. Alicia would need to take extra care of her supplies and spend more time eating berries and whatever else she could gather from her surroundings. That meant no snacks for the cat either; the cougar would have to hunt her own food. If Alicia had luck fishing, then maybe she could share with Tawny, but she didn't know how long she would have to be in this realm. It was better to be safe than sorry.

Alicia packed her things, loaded up her backpack, and walked to the sliver of light hanging in the air. She bent to look through the crack one more time, seeing the distorted image of her parents on the other side.

"I don't know if you can hear me," she said, a lump of sadness in her throat, "but I love you both. I am doing what I can to save you... to save our world. I hope you are okay and not suffering." She choked back a sob. "I may have caused this. But I *promise* I will fix it... somehow."

She stood up, looking at the crack for another moment before turning away. Alicia didn't know what was waiting for her at the hot springs, but regardless, that promise was something she intended to keep.

CH. 12 REVERIE

Alicia spent the morning making her way back to the trail that she had been following since leaving Thunderbolt's mountain the previous day. She turned south, happy to leave the previous night's attack behind her. Alicia found herself disappointed that the area where her cabin would have stood seemed so different in this world, but there was no reason to expect anything else. She was happy to be making progress again after the small detour, and felt that, with no mishaps, she could reach Vulcan by the end of the day at the very latest.

The wandering path took her over low, grass-covered hills before cresting the top of a ridge where the vista opened up, and she had a tremendous view of a long, wide valley below. The forest thinned out in this area, and Alicia could see all the lowlands between here and the mountains on the other side. One of the smaller forks of a river, known as the Salmon River back home, wound its way through the center of the valley. The sun danced along its slow-moving ripples, casting bright sparkles. It looked as if some giant, who perhaps drank a few too many large mugs of mead, had rambled aimlessly across the landscape. The water sparkled like diamonds that might have fallen unnoticed from a hole in the giant's big pack, forming a snaky line from one end of the valley to the other as he tried to avoid falling.

Alicia stood on the ridge watching the river, just for a moment, as it triggered thoughts of her parents who she was so worried about right now. She knew the area well, but had never seen it this green. One of her favorite summer activities was floating down the lazy river on a big inner tube. When she was younger, her dad always went along with her making sure she was safe, even though the river never got very deep or very fast. Thinking about that, a single tear rolled down one cheek which she quickly wiped away. *Stop that!* she told herself.

But this quest she was on kept her deep in thought. For the past couple of years, she had gone without her father, joining some of the older kids from around the lake, including the girl next door. It had given her a sense of independence which she loved. The kids were always careful in the rapids which occasionally presented themselves, and when approaching sections of the river where beavers had dropped trees to block the flow of water, she would paddle to the side and climb out, circling the beaver dam before getting back in downstream.

About two miles down the river from the point where they first entered the water, there was a bridge. It would take a full hour or so to float there, what with their frequent stops to look for snakes or salamanders, but she always knew her dad would be waiting with the car, ready to pick her up and take her home.

Seeing it from this vantage point now, laid out like a sparkling ribbon, Alicia remembered that last float less than a month ago and wondered if she would ever be able to enjoy doing that again.

Not far now, she thought, squinting up at the sun hanging in the sky overhead, wiping her damp forehead. She still had a few miles to go but knew she could get there before night.

Starting down the trail into the valley, she could see Tawny ahead, bounding toward the river. The cat looked like she was hunting. Maybe she spotted one of the rabbits that were common in this area, or maybe she had decided to try and catch her own fish. And maybe she would bring one back for Alicia this time! The girl chuckled at this. *Do I want to eat a fish covered in cat slobber? Yuck!*

She continued to chuckle at that thought as she walked and her mood lightened a bit, giving her the sudden urge to sing. *What was that song I used to sing with my dad?* Alicia thought.

'*Take a moment, look around. See who needs a hand.*' That was it!

'*On this shore where we exist, we're all just grains of sand.*'

She sang softly as she walked, forgetting some of the words and humming those sections instead. She felt good, perhaps the best she'd felt since arriving in this realm. Alicia marveled at the thought. Was it her brush with death the night before that had given her this wonderful feeling of being alive? Or maybe the bond she had formed with the magnificent creature running ahead of her that lightened her spirits? Tawny had protected her like a mother protects a child. Maybe this unusual sense of having a surrogate parent was what filled her with joy today. She didn't know for sure, but whatever it was, she welcomed it and continued to sing.

The song reminded Alicia of Gran'Tree, particularly of her meeting with the yellow pine, which seemed so long ago. In this world, because of the time difference. *It had been a very long time ago.* She thought, when hearing Thunderbolt's story of Gran'Tree's creation, that the tree deserved to be destroyed.

But was that really true? Did anything deserve to be destroyed? Perhaps her good mood made her feel this way, but she didn't think that was why. After all, Gran'Tree hadn't been evil, but he hadn't been remorseful either. Not at first. He was simply trying to live, as all the creatures were.

Magic, not his own by birth, but forced upon him by the power of others, had been the real problem. It had given him a strength he could not control. In the end, he felt sorrow for what he had done to the realm and even cried for the mountain troll, Bristleback. So no, Alicia didn't think he deserved to be destroyed. He only needed to understand. He only needed compassion. She felt that she had given him those things in some small way. She wondered if he was still alive now, and if so, did he still feel compassion?

Alicia made it through the valley and reached the trailhead to the hot springs a couple of hours before nightfall. This offshoot of the main trail continued up into the hills toward the springs, following a small stream along the way. Alicia turned onto this smaller trail and proceeded into the woods to the west, the trees closing in around her.

At some point, Tawny had returned from her roaming, or whatever she had been doing, and was following closely beside the girl. After the open space of the lowlands, Alicia wondered if the cat thought the girl was less protected in the woods themselves, where the trees were denser and there were hidden patches of darkness beneath large bushes. Perhaps she knew that night would be coming soon and wanted to be near, just in case.

The sun fought its way through the branches of the pines, casting torn bits of light on the path. The dirt on the trail here was as fine as talcum powder, maybe an inch thick, and it poofed away in small clouds with each step. Alicia's shoes were soon covered in it, and it turned her socks brown. The dust made her sneeze and she didn't like that, so she tried walking along the very edges of the trail where the dirt seemed to be more packed.

She glanced to the stream, which was formed by a large amount of water coming from the hot springs ahead, meandering along the left side of the trail. As she walked along the path, Alicia would occasionally step over to the water to dip her fingers in, noticing the elevation in temperature each time as she got closer to the source. The rocks in the stream were starting to turn white as well, a build-up of sulfur carried by the hard water and deposited on the stones along its path. The sulfur made the stream smell faintly of eggs, but despite this, she used the water to wash the fine dust off her face.

Alicia and her parents visited Vulcan Hot Springs at least once every summer. They would pack a small picnic of water, sodas, and sometimes wine for her parents, but the best part of the picnic was the hotdogs. The water coming from the springs was boiling hot in some places, heated by the earth's thermal core. In one place, the minerals carried up from deep underground had calcified on either side of the gently erupting water, creating a narrow, deep channel for the water to pass through. Her father would bring a kitchen strainer, place the hotdogs inside, lower the strainer into the flowing water in the small channel, and the hotdogs would cook right there, in nature! To Alicia, that was one of the coolest things ever, cooking in the wild like that with no fire. Somehow, the hotdogs tasted even better when cooked this way. She would slather them in tangy mustard, but no ketchup! She'd gobble down at least two every time.

Thinking about it now, she deeply wished she had some of those hotdogs with her. Grudgingly, she made do with the berries that she gathered during the hike from several of the bushes which were abundant along the sides of the hot springs trail.

The walk along this path to Vulcan was fairly short, only a quarter of a mile or so. The trail had a slight incline all the way as she headed higher into the surrounding hills, but overall it was a pleasant stroll.

In her world, it was common to pass other families along the way. A section of the stream closer to the springs had been blocked off with fallen trees and rocks, making a shallow pool of water ten feet wide, twenty feet long, and two to three feet deep. It was a wonderful, natural place to soak that never got cold. As the hot water filled the pool from upstream at one end, the slightly cooled water poured over the dam of logs and stones at the opposite end in kind of a waterfall to continue its path down to meet up with the bigger river below. Alicia passed the location where the pool would have been in her world and looked longingly at the stream. Sadly, there was no place to soak in this realm. She would have loved to take a real bath and wash away the grime from the days of hiking.

Even though nighttime approached, the air around her was warming, and Alicia knew the hot springs were close. She turned a corner on the trail and looked ahead, the forest opening up before her. Alicia saw a vast empty space. Clouds of steam rose in the evening air, similar to fog, yet somehow more alive, making it impossible to see the far side of the grass-lined clearing.

"We're here, girl!" she said excitedly to the cougar who was following closely behind. "We've reached Vulcan!"

As with Thunderbolt, Alicia had no idea what she would find here and truly hoped to discover answers to her questions. And, more importantly, the solution to the cracks that threatened her world.

CH. 13 VULCAN

Alicia followed the narrow trail forward. It wound along the side of the seemingly empty clearing filled with numerous hot springs. Small holes of various sizes dotted the ground from which hard mineral water boiled up from the depths of the earth to spill onto the land and run down the mountain in a large blanket of heat and steam.

The area was over half the size of a football field, with at least thirty pools of bubbling water. She knew from experience that some of the water was scalding hot, while other pools were only lukewarm. Alicia remembered, as a child, touching one of the hot pools with her finger, against her parents' warnings. Alicia's father took her hand and plunged her scalded fingers into the icy depths of the cooler they had carried in for their picnic. He held them there until the sharp pinpricks of cold surpassed the pain of the burn. The adventurous child felt the burn linger on for the rest of the day but learned her lesson well.

These hot springs did not entirely cover the area with water. The rocky ground was interspersed throughout with dry patches. You could walk out into the rising steam if you stepped carefully, avoiding a myriad of streams which were only an inch or so deep, keeping to the rocks instead.

Alicia dropped her gear in the tall grass and adventured across the rocks, out toward the middle of the springs. She let the steam, more abundant in the cool evening air, envelop her in a cloud of damp warmth. Tawny chose to stay behind with the backpack. The girl guessed that the large cat, much like the house cats back home, preferred to remain dry whenever possible. She did not want the great cat to misstep and burn her huge paws, so it was for the best that she watched from the meadow.

Alicia jumped over small rivulets of hot water, moving from one flat, stony patch to the next, enjoying the warmth of the misty air surrounding her. She didn't have the slightest idea where to start looking for the Ancient that resided here, having never seen any home or dwelling, unlike at Thunderbolt's mountain which had a lookout tower. In this area there was nothing but grasses and wildflowers, and farther back were trees surrounding the hot springs.

Though night came on quickly, she did not feel any sense of urgency to build a fire. Alicia knew from watching the steadily waxing moon on the previous nights that it would be full in the sky tonight, offering plenty of light, and the air was warm enough that she would not feel cold. Without any food to cook, and with a trusted mountain lion to protect her, she could pass the night comfortably without a fire. Tonight, she would enjoy looking at the stars.

As she moved deeper into the hot springs area, steam billowed around her and she lost sight of the sky. There was a wide space in the middle—wide enough to spread out a picnic blanket which her family had done in the past. Reaching it, she sat down, feeling the warm stone beneath her.

"Hellooo," she called softly. For some reason, Alicia always felt this was a place of quiet solitude, a place to commune with nature. When she used to visit with her mom and dad, they always spoke in lower tones, as if any loud sound would disturb the balance of nature in this sacred spot.

No one responded to her call. The only sound was the constant murmur of water—like the hushed voices of an audience before the orchestra begins—not quite as loud as a rushing river, though it would eventually grow louder downstream. Here, where it was born, the sound was softer as if the water, too, respected the sanctity of the location.

As Alicia sat there listening to the sounds of nature, she noticed a stirring in the air around her. Little swirls appeared in the clouds of steam that grew thicker now. She could no longer see to the edge of the hot springs where she assumed Tawny still rested next to the trail. It was like being in a thick fog.

The floating, dancing, multi-colored lights that Alicia had seen in evenings past returned, flitting their way through the dense, warm mist. There were more of them tonight, and though they moved closer than ever, she still could not see them clearly in the cloudy, moist air. The idea of them being will-o'-the-wisps came back. Were these lights everywhere, or did they follow her here? Alternatively, did they *draw* her here? She felt a small chill run down her arms at the thought, despite the heat from the springs.

She saw something larger, humanoid in shape—but ethereal, as if not completely solid—moving through the steam toward her. Alicia rose to her feet and peered more deeply, the shape not yet clear. As she watched, from out of the fog emerged a woman, clearly naked, yet lacking details, like one of the classic carved marble sculptures she had seen in museums at home. Except this sculpture lived.

Alicia's cheeks got hot, and she averted her eyes from embarrassment about the nude figure in front of her. She felt she shouldn't see this powerful being in a state of undress.

"My child." The Ancient facing her spoke as she stepped close and placed a hand on Alicia's cheek. "You do not need to feel shame. Look around you. We are in nature; we are a part of nature. *You* are a part of nature."

Alicia slowly turned her head back toward the woman. "Are...are you...Vulcan?" she asked timidly, already knowing the answer.

For some reason, she could not understand why she felt more in awe of this being than she had been of Thunderbolt. Perhaps it was because he looked more human, if a bit taller than average. He was older, too, and wearing bedclothes, while this being showed no age whatsoever. She appeared timeless, carved into this ivory form. As ageless as the *Venus de Milo*.

"I am, child," she said, lowering her hand. The Ancient's voice was soft and musical, like notes plucked gently on a harp. "And you are Alicia."

The girl smiled and blushed again at being recognized. "I am!" she said. "I am so pleased to meet you."

Her anger at Thunderbolt's cryptic statements and her determination to get answers faded away. She felt at peace in the presence of this being, as if she were a newborn swaddled in her mother's arms.

"I did not expect you to return to this realm," Vulcan said. "You had done what you came to do so long ago. It is time to live your own life."

Steam spun and swirled around the being as she moved closer to the girl. Placing her hands on Alicia's shoulders, she looked warmly at her. "You have your father's eyes."

"You know my dad?" Alicia said with surprise, shocked at the idea that Vulcan had been watching her. This close, she could see very faint streaks of yellowish-orange and red appear on Vulcan's body, dashing up the woman's chest and shoulders in random paths, like flames licking up the side of a burning log.

"I have seen you with Richard," the living statue said. "I have seen him in his boat on the lake. I saw Katie too when you all came to picnic here. Your family seems very happy and loving."

"We are," she agreed. "Or we were, anyway. But now my parents are caught in a time bubble! There are cracks between your world and mine." She paused, pulling away, trying to come up with the right words to explain it. "Your magic is...I don't know...leaking into my world or something. My parents aren't the only ones trapped. I saw squirrels and birds too! I had to return here," she explained, gesturing with her hands, "because it was the only place I knew of where there might be answers."

Alicia turned and paced a few steps away before turning back to the Ancient. "I went to see Thunderbolt first, mostly because he was the closest to where I arrived. But he only gave me more questions. He said he had no magic left."

"Well, almost no magic," Vulcan replied with a gentle laugh. "He did provide you with protection, I see," she said, smiling.

"He said the same thing!" Alicia responded, remembering her conversation with Thunderbolt. "But I don't know what he was talking about. What protection?"

The woman glanced away from the girl, toward the edge of the clearing, seeing something there that was hidden by the steam. "The great beast who follows you. She will give her life for yours."

"Tawny? He gave me Tawny?" Alicia was shocked and amazed. She had been terrified when first seeing the cat, thinking it would kill her, but it hadn't! It came back, night after night. And it *did* protect her from the wolves last night!

"Is that why she is so friendly?" she asked.

"No, child. It is true Thunderbolt sent the cat to you. However, he does not control the beast. He only let her know that you were important and must be protected. Any relationship you form with her is your own doing." Vulcan looked at the girl. "I sent you my own watchers as well."

The living statue sang a high, four-note string, each note drawn out and flowing into the next. The music was unbearably beautiful and brought tears to Alicia's eyes that weren't caused by the steam in the air. She thought she could happily listen to that singing for the rest of her life.

As the notes faded, the floating lights, which had disappeared when Vulcan arrived, returned. One flew in close, alighting on the woman's shoulder, and Alicia stared in fascination. She could now see that it was not simply a lightning bug. It was a small girl. A fairy!

"My sprites have been with you since you first arrived," Vulcan said. "I sent them as soon as I felt your presence here."

Alicia looked at the sprite in wonder. It was *so* tiny, no taller than a pine cone fallen from one of the trees around her cabin. It had the same ivory skin as the Ancient who stood before her, yet it was more crystalline, almost transparent. It had the thinnest wings, like those of a dragonfly, which slowly waved back and forth as it perched on the woman's shoulder.

Alicia lifted her hand and extended an index finger. The sprite looked at the finger for a moment before rapidly beating its wings and flying over to land on the outstretched tip. The creature was light as a feather, and Alicia couldn't help but giggle like a child when it looked up at her with eyes that seemed too big for its tiny head. Those eyes were the softest blue, the same color as the light that emanated from somewhere deep inside the sprite's small body and refracted out through her crystalline skin.

"She is so delicate!" the girl said with a sense of disbelief.

The Ancient watched Alicia with a smile on her face. "They may not have the strength of the mountain lion, but, like her, they have their own will and do not belong to me. I can speak to them, and, with my limited magic, I can see through their eyes."

The sprite took flight again and spun away to join the others that Alicia noticed had gathered around them now. "I saw them," she said, "every night they came. I didn't know what they were. I had never seen them before, even the last time I was here."

"Over four thousand years ago. It's been a long time. You are right; they were not here. They had left during that great catastrophe—The Drying," she explained. "The sprites prefer to spend their time near pockets of water, such as ponds and small lakes. And here, of course," Vulcan gestured toward the springs. "When the great tree took all the water, those pools disappeared, and so the sprites moved on. Since that time—since you saved our realm—they have returned, as have many other forest creatures."

"Other forest creatures?"

"Oh yes, there are many types. Aside from the natural creatures that you already know of—the deer, the squirrels, the wolves—there are magical creatures as well." The Ancient paused, watching the girl take this information in. "Normally, they avoid contact with beings they know little about. The realms have been separated for so long that humans are certainly unknown to them.

"There are the trolls, one of which you already met and befriended." Vulcan's smile dimmed slightly. "Bristleback's cousins have not returned to this land," she said with sadness in her voice, "but the sprites, gnomes, and brownies are back. I even heard tell of a unicorn spotted in the highlands, though I have not seen it myself. They are extremely shy and secretive."

Alicia let her mind wander for a moment, remembering long afternoons spent exploring, and all the secrets she had searched for in these woods her whole young life. She realized now that they *did* exist. A unicorn! She could only dream of meeting such a creature.

Alicia returned to the present and had a sudden panicked thought. While she had been charmed with the small creature on her hand, the Ancient said something she had completely missed, but it came back to her. "Wait...did you say you only have limited magic?"

"I am afraid so, child. We—Thunderbolt and I— gave you the magic you needed to defeat Gran'Tree when we called you here so many years ago." Vulcan looked at Alicia with a combination of affection and sadness. "Just as with him, I have no more magic to give."

"You called me here?" she asked, confused.

"Yes, we allowed you to catch a glimpse through the barrier. You saw and you stepped through. You did what you were born to do."

"Thunderbolt said that same thing—'what I was born to do.' What do you mean by that? I don't understand!" Alicia spun away from the Ancient and stormed to the edge of the dry space, staring into the steam around her. "I don't understand any of it!" Alicia felt a sudden and unexpected anger flood through her, frustrated at learning, once again, that there was no help to be found here.

The circling sprites winked out in response to the girl's anger, slowly and cautiously lighting back up one at a time. Vulcan stepped toward the girl who still stood with her back to the being and rested her hands again on Alicia's shoulders. The angry girl tried to shrug them off, but the Ancient kept them gently, yet firmly, in place.

"Alicia, you have magic in you. You were able to gather a mismatched collection of friends before and keep them around you. I don't understand this type of magic." She turned her head toward the north, to the domain of Thunderbolt. "We prefer solitude. We prefer to avoid each other completely," she explained, referring to the other Ancients, "coming together only when necessary. Even the creatures we work with choose to stay apart from one another." She gestured with one hand to indicate both the group of sprites and the cougar, unseen on the shore. "I haven't seen the Silver King since the creation of the barrier. Since the day that changed everything."

She returned her hand to Alicia's shoulder. "But I can sense him in the earth still. I can sense his power is returning. He will have more than either Thunderbolt or I do. You should go see him."

"Are you kidding?" Alicia pulled away, furious with the woman. Stepping around her, the girl walked back toward the opposite side of the rocky space. Water flowed around the two of them, plotting its course down the mountainside. She spun back toward the naked being and Vulcan could see that behind the anger, Alicia looked very sad and very tired.

"You used me. You 'called' me here, or whatever, to save *your* realm. And now, because of that, *my* realm is in danger." Alicia stared the Ancient in the eyes condemnation in her gaze. "You tried to play God again—you and Thunderbolt. The two of you learned nothing from your past mistakes." She spat the words at Vulcan. "Once again, I am caught up in problems not of my creation." She paused, feeling the fury wash over her. "And now... now *you* say you can't help me. You're sending me away, washing your hands of me, just like Thunderbolt did!"

"Alicia, there are things you do not know," Vulcan started.

"So tell me!" Alicia interrupted. "Wait, you know what? Don't! Don't say any more. You've wasted my time. Both of you have. He said I'd get answers here. But you've done *nothing* for me."

The girl turned away from the Ancient, leaving a shocked and saddened look on Vulcan's porcelain features. "I'm leaving," Alicia growled. "I'm going to find the Silver King. At least he was smart enough to stay away while you two could not leave well enough alone." She stepped across the streams of hot water, moving away through the warm fog. "You say you can feel his powers through the stone?" she called over her shoulder as she continued toward the meadow. "Maybe he got them back. He was always the strongest," she taunted. "Perhaps he will help me."

Only silence followed her. Alicia reached the edge of the springs, emerging from the steam to see the great cat pacing back and forth along the shore. She must have sensed Alicia's frustration.

"It's okay, girl. I'm okay. Just angry, that's all." She wanted to scratch the cougar between the ears, but didn't feel quite that comfortable with the beast yet. And in the cat's agitated state, Alicia didn't know if it would bite or not.

"Come on; we're leaving," she told Tawny.

Alicia looked back into the steam of the hot springs, but could no longer see the Ancient. She shrugged on her backpack and started back down the path to the main trail, no longer wanting to be here, even with the warmth the springs provided. She would find another place to spend the night—away from the being that used her. Was she still being used? She didn't know. But as she looked to the future and her meeting with the Silver King, she knew without a doubt that he was her last hope.

CH. 14 INTO DARKNESS

Alicia and Tawny spent the night in darkness. The frustrated teenager was in no mood to build a fire to provide light, but the moon hovering in the sky offered a soft white glow. Quickly, she turned on her flashlight to lay out a blanket and select food for dinner, but, for fear of the batteries going dead, she didn't keep the light on.

"Thank you for keeping me company," she said to the silent cougar. "I know Thunderbolt sent you to watch out for me, but you could have done that from a distance." She let out a heavy sigh. "Now you are the only real friend I have here."

The great cat looked at the girl and gave no response, except for a slow blink, which Alicia took as a good sign. She doubted the cat could actually understand her words. Perhaps the magic she had *did* help her bond with the wildland creatures.

The sprites didn't show up that night. It could be she angered Vulcan by leaving in a huff, and so the being told them to leave the human be. Or, maybe, as the Ancient said, they just didn't play nicely with the cougar and chose to stay away. Alicia once again arranged her pack like a pillow and fell asleep listening to the sounds of Tawny breathing.

The morning dawned quickly, warm and bright. Alicia awoke thinking about her encounter with Vulcan. She began to regret fleeing so quickly, but the Ancient had said she had no magic to give, so why should Alicia waste time?

Standing and brushing her jeans, she grabbed her spear and tramped off to the nearby stream to fish. She wasn't hungry herself, but thought Tawny might appreciate a fish for breakfast, and she wanted to say thank you for not leaving during the night. Alicia knew the cat could hunt for herself, but in some way, she felt her actions were a way of deepening their bond.

She speared a river trout quickly and tossed it to Tawny, who had followed her and now waited patiently nearby. The cougar devoured the fish quickly, taking large bites, and looked back at the girl as if to say, "Is that all?"

"Sorry, girl. You'll have to wait until later or find something yourself. I'm running low on jerky, but I'm done fishing for now."

Tawny looked at her a moment longer with that expressionless stare, revealing nothing about what she might be thinking, before turning away and heading toward the stream to lap up the flowing water.

Alicia retrieved her backpack. The trail was uphill from her campsite and would be a tiring trek, but she only had a few miles to go before reaching the mine where she assumed the king lived.

The Eureka Silver King Mine had closed down many years ago, long before she was born. It was not the only mine in the area, but it was the closest.

In her world, there was a gold mine thirty miles away, near the small town of Yellow Pine, and she knew that mine was still active. Alicia had visited the rustic town once a few years ago for the harmonica festival they held there. *I'll have to visit again,* she thought. *That is, if there is anything to go back to.*

Picking up her walking stick, Alicia continued her journey south. The mountain lion had finished drinking and followed after, not quite keeping pace with the girl, but doing her own thing instead and wandering out among the trees. *Doing whatever large cats do*, Alicia thought as she watched the cougar roam.

The girl trudged along, replaying the conversation with Vulcan in her head. She was still surprised to learn that the Ancient knew of her mom and dad, and that she had watched Alicia and her family without their knowledge, and continued to do so now with the sprites. Thinking about it gave her the creeps! And, once again, she had been told that she had magic, but nobody seemed to be able to tell her what that magic was, or how to use it.

Could she fly? That would be so cool! And it sure would have made this trek a lot easier. Alicia didn't really think she could fly or turn invisible or walk through walls, but who knew what powers she possessed. Maybe it was possible. After all, there might be a horse with a horn running around somewhere in this forest. If unicorns were real, then maybe flying humans could be real too!

She laughed at the thought of a bunch of people flying around in the sky.

"Hey, Joe, where are you headed?"

"Going out to pick up some donuts for the office. How about you?"

"Oh, my son forgot his homework at home, so I'm...you know...flying it over."

"Okay, see ya later. Watch out for that...
OUCH...pigeon..."

"HA HA HA!" Alicia bellowed aloud at the idea, causing Tawny to come closer to find out if there was any trouble. Seeing nothing threatening, just the girl making noises and holding her belly, the cat disappeared back into the forest to return to her exploration.

Alicia's laughter improved her mood, as it always did. Feeling calmer, she returned to thinking about her "magic." She still had no idea what it could be. The creatures here kept referring to love as if that was a foreign thing, something they don't understand. Could that be true? By using their powers not for good, but to create a barrier that banished the human race, perhaps the Ancient Ones had banished love from this land as well.

She considered that idea—which didn't make sense to her—but maybe that was it! And maybe what the creatures saw as magic was actually her ability to love and spread love to others. Alicia remembered how, during her last trip to the Wild Side, her friends—the squirrel, the jay, and the deer—were drawn to her—even the mountain troll. They all said it was because of the feeling of being a family, something they'd never felt before. Maybe it was more than that. Not at first, of course, but that sense of love that they had never experienced, maybe that was the glue that bound them all together.

She thought back to Gran'Tree. In the end, he was filled with such emotion by her song that it overwhelmed him. Perhaps it was an emotion that he had never felt before, which was why it consumed him so completely. Could it really be as simple as that? *Love.* Could that be it?

The idea seemed a bit silly to her at first, but the more she thought about it, the more it felt right. After all, when you give love, you get it in return. And her natural instinct of loving all living creatures—something instilled in her at a young age by her parents—could have been all that her friends, and even Gran'Tree, needed to feel. That special feeling of being loved allowed loving others to blossom within them. Had she planted a seed that bloomed inside them all?

Alicia decided she liked the thought and would hold onto this idea in the hopes that, in time, it would make the many mysteries she faced become clearer.

With a lightened heart, she continued her journey to the final Ancient.

Alicia looked into the black maw of the cave and saw the remnants of mine cart tracks, built ages ago, which started a few feet inside and continued into the darkness.

She had already made camp not far from the mine's entrance. It took her most of the day to reach this area, and she did not want to get stuck in the same situation as the night before. After her disappointing talk with Vulcan, it was already so late that she no longer had the time or energy to set anything up properly. So today she chose a spot, gathered and arranged rocks for a fire pit, and found a place to leave her belongings *before* setting out to meet this Ancient.

Alicia supposed she could have waited until morning to meet the Silver King, but felt impatient after two false starts and was ready to be done with all of this. She brought only her flashlight and her walking stick with her to the cave.

Dreading what may happen, she stared into the inky darkness of the old mine. Water filled the floor of the tunnel, its glossy black surface making it impossible to tell how deep the ditch really was. The entrance was so small she would have to crouch to enter or risk bumping her head on the weathered wood beam that supported the opening. Using her walking stick, Alicia poked the tip into the water, checking its depth. The stick sank only a couple of inches. *Not bad*, she thought. *I can deal with having wet shoes for a bit.*

Looking into the cobweb-filled cave, she shivered. Alicia had never been squeamish about most bugs and other creepy crawlies. Even as a child, she would find the most fascinating beetles with irides-cent shells to bring home to her parents. Spiders, however, were another story. While not exactly fearful of the eight-legged creatures, she preferred to avoid them whenever possible. Peering into the gloom ahead of her, Alicia was barely able to make out the nooks and crannies that would be perfect hiding spots for them. She would have to be extra careful not to brush up against the walls as she walked, hunched over, into the depths of the mine.

"Okay," she said out loud, psyching herself up and setting her walking stick aside, "let's get moving." Alicia stepped into the water and, after a second or two, felt the shockingly cold wetness penetrate her sock, instantly freezing her ankle to the bone. Tawny watched this disinterestedly from her resting spot in the dirt nearby, not deigning to get her paws wet.

Turning on her flashlight, Alicia shined it into the mine, but the dust-speckled beam was not strong enough to reach the end of the tunnel. Making her way through was *not* going to be fun. Thankfully, the water was shallow and, as she continued to move forward, her feet became numb to the cold rather quickly.

As she journeyed farther away from the opening, the light around her slowly dimmed. The sound of the woods from outside, a constant orchestra of noises, grew quieter and quieter, while the *slosh,*

slosh of water swirling at her feet echoed off the narrow walls. The air felt clammy the farther she moved from the entrance as the air became colder and mustier. The atmosphere was the exact opposite of her experience at Vulcan's hot springs.

She could feel the hard metal of the mine cart tracks against her feet and tried to avoid stepping on them for fear of slipping, staying centered between them as much as possible.

There were thick wooden pillars, which reached from floor to ceiling, evenly spaced down the tunnel. In the evenings, while the family gathered around the fire, her grandfather would tell old stories about the mine. He'd said that these columns supported the tunnel walls and kept them from collapsing. She hoped against hope that they were still strong enough to do that.

Alicia continued moving slowly and quietly, listening to the rhythmic sounds of water splashing with each footfall through the flooded tunnel. It was much darker now and she glanced behind her. The entrance to the mine in the distance looked as though it had shrunk to the size of a quarter, and she could see the faint outline of Tawny's head. The cougar must've gotten curious and was watching her as she trudged away. *Wow, I'm in here deep!* Looking forward, she noticed what appeared to be a bend in the tunnel at the far reaches of her flashlight beam. Maybe she was close!

Suddenly, Alicia's shoe caught on something underwater—perhaps a loose part of the mine cart track—and she stumbled forward. She quickly put out a hand to catch herself from falling, grabbing at one of the support logs along the wall. Her hand met what appeared to be a solid surface, but sank into the old log as if the wood was made out of a stick of butter left on the kitchen counter overnight. Centuries of water and time had aged and softened the wood until it was nothing more than a pillar-shaped tower of rotten muck. Her hand sank all the way through the beam, finally coming to a halt against the wall of the mine, stopping her fall. She straightened quickly and pulled her hand out of the muck. Fear crept into her mind as she realized the beams no longer supported the ceiling, that at any time, the roof could come crashing down on her head.

Panic gripped Alicia's heart as she rinsed her muddy hand in the cold water around her feet. She wanted more than anything to flee the confines of this dark tunnel for the safety of the outside world, but knew she had to speak with the Silver King. Reluctantly, she struggled onward, further down the ancient mine shaft.

Alicia reached the bend in the tunnel and turned the corner. She paused, shining the light down this new corridor, but it looked much the same as the one she just left, and her light did not travel far enough for her to see the end. Though she knew it was terribly unsafe, she continued on, determined to see this through. The thought of the roof collapsing and burying her forever made her less cautious than before, and she hurried more recklessly. She thought of Tawny waiting outside, not daring to enter the wet cave. Maybe now she understood part of the cat's unwillingness.

Alicia noticed that the path she was on started descending into a downhill slope, causing the water to become deeper the farther she progressed. All source of light from the entrance had disappeared around the bend, and she could no longer hear any sounds but the echoes of the water, which was now as high as her knees and rising with each step forward.

"Brrr, this is really cold!" she exclaimed out loud, and heard the words echo back to her. *Cold... cold... cold...* Those words sounded eerie and distorted and brought with them their own chill, one that was sensed more than physically felt. Alicia decided to keep her thoughts inside her head for the time being; speaking them out loud seemed to bring them to life.

The water level had risen enough that Alicia now stood waist-deep, requiring her to raise her arms to keep them dry and the flashlight safe. She felt something wriggle past her and hoped it was only one of the garter snakes that were common in these woods. They were not poisonous and certainly wanted nothing to do with this stranger invading their domain.

Alicia took another step forward and had the sudden sensation of weightlessness as she felt empty space beneath her foot. She realized her error too late, letting fear guide her steps too quickly. There was some sort of hole in the cave floor ahead of her! Before she could react, she lost her balance, plunging forward until her head and body were completely submerged under the freezing water of this unknown place.

Alicia thrashed frantically for a moment. She was a good swimmer, but the darkness and the cold disoriented her. A primal terror set in as she struggled to tell which way was up and how to reach safety. She didn't want to drown here in this abandoned mine, far from her world, far from her parents and friends. No one but the cougar knew where she was. She felt her lungs straining and feared that this was the end.

Suddenly, there was solid ground beneath her. Alicia planted her feet and, using all of her strength, pushed up, forcing her head through the surface of the water. She saw nothing but blackness all around. The fall, in reality, was a trip that dropped her no more than a few feet, but the blackness had been disorienting enough to make it seem like much more. She was standing upright; the level of the water was now almost up to her neck. Worse than that, however, her flashlight went under too. She lifted it, feeling the water stream down its sides and across her fingers, and her worst fear was confirmed—she had no light.

The darkness enveloped Alicia so completely that she could not see her hand in front of her face. She blinked several times, as if the gloom were a physical substance sticking to her eyeballs that could be cleared away. The cold claws of anxiety gripped her fiercely as she shook the flashlight, distressed by its inability to shine. She slapped it hard against her free hand, trying in vain to resuscitate it and get more life out of the old batteries. There was a faint flicker, a hopeful spark, and then it was gone. No amount of beating on the light was going to bring it back.

Alicia stopped shaking the light, her shoulders sinking in despair. She stood alone in a dark, dank hole that she might never escape from. She breathed in short, sharp bursts, struggling to control it as fear welled inside, but her involuntary gasps wouldn't stop. *Calm, calm*, she thought to herself, searching for the strength to deal with this situation.

She closed her eyes and continued to repeat the word like a mantra. Ever so slowly, her breathing returned to normal, and Alicia thought about her options—she could turn back now, *should* turn back now. She hadn't seen any branches on the tracks, so she could move slowly with extended hands to guide her until she found the bend. Once she turned that corner, she should be able to see the opening in the distance. She'd find her way out without the flashlight, Alicia was sure of it. But then what? She had reached a dead end in her search for answers and needed help. She needed the Silver King.

It was terrifying to consider, but she felt compelled to move forward. There was no other option. *But what if there is another drop like the one I just had?* Swimming through a black cave was not an idea she relished. On top of that, the water was so terribly cold that she could feel her bones aching!

Squeezing her eyes even more tightly shut against the darkness, Alicia let out a scream of rage and frustration. The shout carried off into the distance, filling the mine with sound and echoing all around her. She stood there with her eyes closed, coming to terms with her next move. Eventually, Alicia reached her right hand out until it brushed the damp wall, then she did the same with her left. If she stretched her arms and fingers as far as they could go, she could touch both walls at the same time.

"Okay," she spoke to herself, "you can do this. Keep your hands brushing the walls on either side. If you feel an opening of any kind, a branching path, you need to turn around. It would be too easy to get lost in here."

She would give herself a little more time to explore. In reality, she could always leave and return with some sort of torch. A long stick wrapped in... what? She didn't know—maybe her blanket if it came to that. Now that she was aware of the drop, she would be prepared for it and could lower herself over the edge, keeping the torch held high so it couldn't get doused.

With a plan in mind, Alicia opened her eyes and noticed a light. The faintest glow hovered at the very limits of her vision, floating high above her in the distance.

She stared at the light, wondering if she imagined it. It could be an aftereffect of closing her eyes so tightly, or just an illusion that would fade in a moment. She continued to focus on it, trying to let her eyes adjust, but when the light didn't fade, a spark of hope lit within her.

Alicia pushed forward, more carefully now that she had no flashlight, but with renewed urgency, fighting the chest-high water. The dim light ahead grew increasingly brighter as she progressed, reflecting off of the water and flashing on the wet walls that surrounded her. She kept her arms extended, her fingers carving small grooves in the mud of the walls. After several more yards, she could feel the ground rising under her feet, each step taking her into shallower water.

With a great heave of her sodden shoes, she at last took a squelching step up out of the water onto dry soil. She could see the ground ahead of her slope upward toward and through the ceiling. It appeared that a mine collapse had occurred here at some time in the past, raining down dirt and debris which had formed this huge mound in front of her, creating a climbable hill. She could see the opening above belonging to another passage, and through the hole, a large chamber was barely visible, obviously the source of the light.

Alicia clambered up the slope, using her hands to dig in and pull herself higher, eager to get away from the water and the darkness below. The light grew brighter, and with a final lunge, she pulled herself into a new passage.

Alicia rested on her hands and knees for a moment, catching her breath. When she raised her head, she froze in disbelief about what she saw. The room before her looked massive enough to be the size of a small movie theater. The ceiling stood so far above, it was almost lost in darkness. Despite the grandeur of the room, her eyes were drawn to what stood in front of her. It was an enormous deposit of silver, polished and glinting, a small mountain of it here within this room.

Alicia slowly stood, studying the great mound of metal. The silver had a smooth, blobby, amorphous look, as if something huge—a mountain troll perhaps—had taken a giant utensil and dripped heaping spoonfuls of mercury, one after the other, each clump freezing in place where it landed. The drops had formed a hollow in the middle, a depression the shape of a large chair or throne. And on that throne sat the statue of what appeared to be a man, carved from dirt and mud.

"Hello, my dear," the statue said. "Welcome to my domain. Come closer."

As she watched, surprise plastered across her face, the mud man sat forward and raised an arm, beckoning.

Alicia realized then that she stood in the presence of the Silver King.

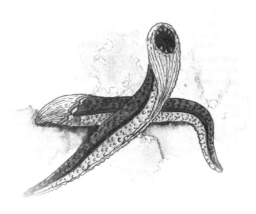

CH. 15 THE SILVER KING

Alicia stumbled forward, staring at the Ancient before her—a being of mud and decay. He had been the most powerful of all the beings in this realm before they had used their terrible power to sever the worlds. She walked hesitantly toward the throne.

As she approached, her eyes scanned the magnificent room around her. What appeared to be black vines—some type of cave moss—hung from the ceiling like strands of wet hair. The air was heavy with the smell of dirt, not the pleasant aroma of the wet earth after a rain, but the sour stench of rot and mud.

Alicia could see tiny cracks in the roof of the chamber where small rays of sunlight filtered in, glinting off the silver throne, reflecting crazily in different directions. This was the source of the light she had seen earlier. While not enough to completely banish the darkness, it was bright enough to allow her to see the dark features of the king.

"It's been an age since someone has visited me here." His voice was wet and phlegmy, like gases rising through a swamp, only to burst in the air and release their words. "And there have been no humans in this realm since we put up the barrier. How did you come to be here?"

Alicia looked in amazement at this being, so primeval. He was larger than a normal man, and his body—formed from the earth—was not clearly defined. It appeared as if time had done to him exactly what it had done to the sodden wooden pillars in the passage. His features drooped slightly as he spoke. She wondered if her hand would sink into his skin as well if she touched him.

"Hello, sir, uh, your majesty, uh..." she fumbled not knowing what to call him.

"Come now, there is no need for formalities," he burped muddily back at her, settling into his massive chair. "Tell me your name. Tell me what is happening in the world above."

She struggled to pull herself together, feeling wet and dirty, not worthy of standing in the presence of a king, regardless of his slumped appearance.

"It is a bit of a long story, sir," she began. "My name is Alicia. I came to this world three years ago. Well, four thousand years ago by your time. I don't quite understand how, but the other Ancients said they 'called' to me."

The Silver King made a disgusting sound with his lips. "Those two," he said. "Continuing to disturb the balance after everything we did."

"I know!" the girl blurted out, immediately feeling embarrassed by her outburst. "I know," she repeated in a softer tone. "I said the same thing. I mean, I sort of understand their reasons, trying to defeat Gran'Tree and all."

"Gran'Tree?" the king interrupted with the question.

"You don't know about Gran'Tree?" Alicia was perplexed. "Wait. After you created the barrier, you returned here and never left this mine!"

"The underworld is my home, even after your kind destroyed this mountain." Anger filled his voice and, with it, a low rumble reverberated through the ground under Alicia's feet. She threw out her hands to keep her balance, seeing the vines swaying above her head. She was fearful of a possible cave-in. "This mine remains my home. I have no need to leave!"

The rumble diminished, but Alicia could sense this earth being had power—more power than the other two Ancients, a thought which gave her hope.

"Gran'Tree was a great yellow pine, bigger than any tree before it. You actually had a hand in creating it."

"I did nothing of the sort," the Silver King argued. "What makes you think I had anything to do with that? Did those *others*," he spat the word as if he had tasted something foul, "tell you that *I* did something?"

Alicia didn't want to anger the king any more than he already appeared to be, but she pushed on. "When you all created the barrier, there was a seed, unseen by any of you. That pine seed absorbed some of your strength—some strength from all three of you. It wasn't your fault, exactly," she said, trying to take some of the sting out of her words, "but that seed grew into the great tree that stretched as high as the heavens. The tree almost destroyed this realm with its desire to become the biggest and the strongest. It sucked most of the water from the land."

"I remember my tunnels growing drier," the old king said. "But that was so long ago."

"Yes," she agreed. "It was over four thousand years in your time. I came through the barrier." Alicia could not stop herself from sharing the story

Thunderbolt shared. "Thunderbolt and Vulcan said they gave me the power to defeat Gran'Tree. They also said I had power within me." She felt her heart beating in her throat and swallowed, hoping to push it back where it belonged. "I don't know if that's the same thing or something greater. But I found the great tree. I spoke to him. I sang to him. And in the end, he gave back all that he had stolen from the lands." She caught her breath and felt a smile grow on her face. She was hopeful now that this Ancient may actually be able to help her.

"You *do* have power in you," the Silver King said, a note of eagerness creeping into his voice. He leaned forward once again, examining the girl. "I can sense it now. Something I haven't felt in a long, long time." Vibrations stirred through the earth again, smaller than before, but noticeable.

"I was able to cross back. I don't know how, but everything seemed fine," Alicia continued. "And now, three years later in my world, there are cracks appearing in the barrier between our realms." She had to make sure the Silver King understood the severity of the situation she faced. "The flow of time from the two sides is conflicting somehow, creating these bubbles of frozen time. My...my parents are trapped in one. I have come here because I need your help." Her furrowed brow replaced the smile from only moments ago, while sharing the truth about her parent's situation.

The Silver King looked her up and down. She felt self-conscious about her appearance, knowing she must resemble a drowned rat, and avoided his gaze. "I thought I felt a shifting, a tremor across creation," he said. "I didn't know what it could be, but I have little concern anymore for the events in the world above. I left that world after the severing of the realms."

The king leaned back in his throne. Alicia watched the being made of mud. "So much time, I have been waiting down here in the dark with only my pets for company," he contemplated, "waiting for my energy to return. I know nothing of what happens up there," he gestured to the ceiling with his eyes.

"Did you know this mine used to be bustling with activity?" he asked, remembering back to a happier time. "There were men coming and going all day and night. They would talk to me here in the dark, tell me stories, and give me gifts of silver. And I ruled over it all!" The king's voice turned sour. "But you humans were greedy, and the gifts stopped coming. You started to take and take, never giving; you took all my beloved silver. We *had* to create a barrier to protect what was ours."

The king leaned forward again, staring intently at Alicia; she could see herself in his eye. "That creation sapped me of my strength. So now, here I live. Alone. Down in the dark with the bugs and the snakes, never knowing what became of the world of light." He snarled wetly, accusingly. As he spoke, the rumbling came and went again.

Alicia looked at the king apprehensively. "Does that mean you can't help me?" she asked, fearing the answer.

"My power has come back slowly. Ever so slowly," he replied, leaning back against his throne once again. "What I have sustains me now. Why should I use it to help you—a human? If I were to help you, what would become of me? Why should I care about your world or your family?" He looked down at the girl in front of him. "If I were to help you, what would you give me in return?"

Alicia held her arms out to her sides, palms forward. In one hand she held the useless flashlight, and the other was empty. "I have nothing to give, sir," she replied, the sorrow in her voice echoed the helplessness in her heart.

"Oh, but you do," the king said, a muddy smile slowly growing on his face. "I do sense a power in you, my dear. But it seems buried, hidden."

"I don't feel the power," she said, dejectedly. "I'm as useless as this flashlight now." She held up the dead flashlight, looking past the Ancient, her hopeful glow as extinguished as the light stick in her hand.

"Maybe I can do something to help you release it," the Silver King said, a renewed desire in his voice. "Maybe if I do that, you can share your power with me." His voice rose, growing louder in the large chamber. "Or maybe...I can take it for myself!"

Alicia didn't like those words or the tone that had crept into the old being's voice. She took a step back from the king, creating distance between the two of them.

"My pets will feed well tonight," he whispered and snapped his fingers with a wet squelch. The vibrations returned to the earth, growing stronger and throwing the girl off balance.

"What are you doing?" she cried. "Stop, please!"

The vibrations continued, and Alicia noticed movement out of the corner of her eye. Glancing up, she saw that the hanging vines appeared more active than when she entered the cave, as if a strong wind was blowing across their surface causing them to ripple like a field of wheat turned upside down. As she watched, one of the vines fell, knocked loose by the rumbling that filled the cavern. It landed on the ground in front of her, and, to her utter surprise, began undulating toward her. It was black, shiny, and moist, and as it moved toward her, it stretched and retracted, stretched and retracted, propelling itself forward with each movement like a monstrous caterpillar. Alicia squinted in the dim light and looked closer at the thing approaching her. With horror, she realized what she had mistaken for cave vines in the dark were something much more terrible and frightening.

Leeches.

They began dropping, one after the other, from the wet ceiling—thousands of them!

Alicia backed slowly away from the Silver King, her eyes darting left and right as more of the leeches detached themselves from the ceiling, coming down like the darkest rain imaginable.

"Why are you doing this?!" she screamed at the king. She felt something hit her head and reached up to find one of the large creatures squirming through her hair, searching for her scalp. She pulled it from her head and stared as it writhed frantically in her fingers. The leech looked like a fat, black earthworm, except for both ends which had suckers for tips. The end closest to her, the head, had the largest sucker, and she could see a small hole in the middle. That was the mouth, where the needle-like proboscis would extend to draw blood from her scalp. She screamed and flung the horrible creature as far from her as she could.

Another of the disgusting worms landed on her neck and immediately sank its mouthparts into her skin, piercing the flesh and feasting on her warm, delicious blood.

Alicia reached back and grasped the squirming thing, which was slippery and covered in mucus, and it continued to suck as she unsuccessfully tried to grip it. Finally, she slid a ragged fingernail between the mouthpiece of the leech and her skin, prying it away and feeling a line of blood run down the back of her neck. She threw the thing to the ground at her feet, stomping on it and feeling a satisfying *squish*.

The Silver King watched and laughed, his voice filled with malevolence. "Don't worry, my dear, they are small and don't eat much. But there are so many, and we are so hungry. They will give me your power!" His evil laughter continued to echo around the cavern.

Alicia turned and fled, plunging blindly down the steep slope into the chamber below. She lost her footing and tumbled head over heels until she landed with a splash in the water. The darkness of the mine passage wrapped her in its heavy weight as she left behind the dim light of the audience chamber, the king, and his foul pets. The water in the tunnel immediately soaked her, and she felt the icy cold like razors on her skin. The deep water slowed her progress, but she pushed forward as hard as she could, hearing the slipping sound of thousands of leeches trailing her closely. They slid across one another, plopping into the water behind her and blindly searching for the girl, sensing the warmth of her body and craving the blood pumping within.

"Get her!" she heard the Silver King scream from behind her. The tunnel rumbled violently around her, the muddy water splashing into her eyes.

"Feed. FEED! RELEASE THE MAGIC!! GIVE IT TO MEEE!!!"

The leeches, faster now that they were in the water, stretched their rubbery bodies to full length and undulated through the dark like small eels. They piled into the water behind her, sensing her movements up ahead with the almost invisible, hair-like protrusions that covered their bodies.

Alicia continued her flight, arms outstretched ahead of her in the blackness of the old mine. She tried to pick up her feet as much as possible with each step because she knew if she tripped and went down now, the hungry creatures would be all over her in a heartbeat, biting, sucking, draining her life-sustaining blood.

In the deep water of this tunnel, the leeches moved more quickly than she could, and Alicia was losing the head start she had gained with her initial burst of speed as she tumbled down the hill. She knew that if she could get to the bend in the tunnel, the water would grow shallower and she would be able to see the light at the entrance for guidance.

Alicia felt a wriggling on her left ankle, followed by the stab of a leech attaching itself there. They had reached her. Seconds later, she felt another stab alongside the first. Alicia fought harder to move forward, pulling what energy she had left from deep inside of her, feeling a third stab on her right ankle and a fourth on the back of her arm. She started to lose count, and terror consumed her as more and more leeches found her bare skin and began to feast.

Struggling forward, ignoring the grotesque worms dangling from her skin, Alicia kept her arms outstretched in front, and periodically to her left and right, to help guide her by feeling for the walls. Her knee collided with the edge where she had fallen off before, sending a strong jolt of pain racing up her leg. Doing her best to ignore it, she scrambled up the small ledge and the water dropped away to her waist. She could move more rapidly now, though still slower than she wanted. She knew the bend was up ahead—not too much farther. That knowledge gave her hope.

Feeling another leech swimming up her pant leg and attaching its sucker-like mouth to her skin, Alicia knew she still wasn't safe and slogged forward as hard as she could. Her breath came in huge gasps as she gradually made her way up the slope, feeling the water becoming shallower. Suddenly, her out-stretched hands sank into the muddy wall ahead of her, and she turned left toward the main entrance and escape.

Far in the distance, she could see the opening to the mine, but the light it had provided earlier was less pronounced. How long had she been in the cavern? Night was falling which made the light in the passage dim rapidly.

The water was only ankle deep at this point, and she ran toward the entrance, caution thrown to the wind. Leeches dangled from her arms and legs, drinking and swelling with blood, their middle sections becoming round as if they were small, disgusting balloons slowly inflating with air.

Darker and darker the tunnel became as she raced to the exit, trying desperately to outrun the setting of the sun. The mud on the floor sucked at her shoes with each step, but still, she ran. She no longer heard the cruel, hungry laughter of the Silver King, but the underground tremors continued. She knew that if she slowed, the pursuing leeches could still reach her.

Alicia burst from the mine entrance and saw Tawny there, first looking questioningly at her and then looking back with alarm toward the tunnel to see what chased her. Alicia just kept running, leaving the great cat no choice but to follow. She needed to put as much distance as possible between her, the mine, and the dark horrors that hid there.

CH. 16 FAMILY NOW

Alicia hadn't stopped running until she arrived back at her camp, and by then night had fully descended. The cougar paced her the entire way, frequently looking back over its shoulder in confusion, unable to determine what chased them, and wondering why the girl was so focused on running.

Ignoring the leeches on her for the moment, Alicia quickly gathered the dead branches and materials she had collected earlier in the day, throwing them into the rock circle she had created. She was freezing wet and needed to get a fire going before she could even think about anything else.

Alicia pulled the box of matches from her pack and quickly started a warm blaze, larger than she had built on previous nights. Only then did she sit down on a large log and go to work pulling the leeches off one by one, depositing them none too gently into the flames. She counted thirteen in total. Standing, she stripped off her wet clothes and searched her skin by the light of the fire to make sure there were no more hiding out of sight. Thin ribbons of blood streamed down her arms and legs from the wounds left behind by the worms.

Alicia scraped the final leech from her arm and flung it into the fire. Hearing it sizzle and watching the smoke rise from the curling body gave her a sense of relief. She knew some of her blood burned and smoked there as well, and almost felt bad for the foul creature, but she was exhausted and upset from her encounter with the Silver King. Sadly, there was little room for compassion in a mind filled with anger.

Alicia took her wet clothes and draped them over a spot on the log where the heat of the fire would dry them. Pulling her blanket out of her pack, she wrapped it around her body and sat back down on the log. She looked over at her guardian—the great cat.

Tawny gave a long stretch and growl, spreading herself to full length beside the fire, and raised her eyes to the girl. "You are so lucky you didn't follow me in there," Alicia told the cat. "There was more than just cold water and wet feet. I don't think you could have protected me from what was inside. I don't even want to think about it!"

Alicia shuddered from more than just the cold and found herself unable to stop shaking. She stood and pulled her makeshift seat even closer to the fire, hoping the warmth could drive away the lingering terror inside.

She felt a tickle on her neck and reached quickly back to grab whatever lurked there, but it was only a drop of water sliding down from her still wet hair. Realizing this, Alicia finally burst into great sobs. The sobs carried within them relief at having escaped the evil king's domain, but also hopelessness about the situation she currently found herself in.

What was she to do now? At this moment, she felt small and fragile, like one of Vulcan's sprites. It seemed like she could only watch events unfold around her, with no control of anything, like a bug on a leaf being swept down a river. At any moment, she expected some great metaphorical fish to leap out of the rapids and devour her. She couldn't stop thinking about the fact that she barely escaped literally being eaten alive today.

Alicia had counted on the Ancient Ones being able to help her, and the Silver King had been her last hope. She imagined he must have been a great ruler at one point watching over his underground kingdom of ore, but his bitterness at losing his strength as he banished human subjects from the realm had taken over. He lost all signs of kindness, leaving behind a soul that matched the rotten mud that he had become. Now he only craved the power that he had lost.

The heat from the campfire finally warmed her body, casting flickering light across her face and drying the tears there. As Alicia's crying diminished, she thought about what she saw in the great Ancients. *Greed.* That was the underlying cause of all the problems she now found herself facing. It had begun with humans' greed and desire for expansion at all costs—the thing that had forced the Ancients to create the barrier, which in turn created Gran'Tree. The giant tree's greedy desire for water and all the power it granted him almost destroyed the realm of magic, leading to Thunderbolt and Vulcan calling her to the Wild Side in the first place. The barrier had cracked as a side effect of Gran'Tree's greed, trapping her parents, and potentially countless others, in those pockets of frozen time.

And now, the only being left with any significant power was the Silver King, but the greed within him caused him to refuse to share precious resources. He would not give her a bit of his power which might help free her parents and seal the barrier once again. Stronger than ignorance, stronger than jealousy, stronger even than hate, greed was the most destructive force in the world. She was sure of it.

Alicia used a corner of the blanket to wipe the last of her tears away. What had the king said about her power? That she still had some within her—it was hidden, yet alive. Could she somehow tap into that? Sadly, she didn't know how!

Closing her eyes, she allowed the warmth of the flames to calm her. She could still see the firelight flickering through her closed eyelids and focused on that, letting the rest of the world vanish.

Her mind turned inward, and Alicia searched for the power within. Her thoughts traveled through each limb, through her fingers and toes, through her stomach, her lungs, and finally, to her heart. Could she feel anything special there? As she searched, she became aware of *something*. It wasn't a thing she could see with her mind's eye, but she felt something. What was it? Suddenly, she remembered the brief song that Vulcan had sung calling the sprites to her. It was so beautiful, so mesmerizing. Alicia had done that with the great tree, but hadn't meant to, exactly. It just happened. Was that her magic? The power of song?

Alicia slowly opened her eyes and saw the cougar watching her. Hope was not gone. There might be one being left who had witnessed her magic, who had seen it firsthand and had been moved by it. Might he know? She dreaded the thought of traveling there, of facing that monster again. After all, she had stripped him of his strength. In some odd way, though, she wasn't surprised that her journey led her to this.

Alicia, exhausted from the events of the day, laid down on her side by the fire, watching the flames slowly die into glowing coals. Smoke curled lazily into the dark sky like long gray ribbons, and small sparks rose a few feet from the dying fire before winking out. She still had not seen the sprites return, but the cat never left her side once the sky began to darken.

She heard Tawny stir. The cougar came up behind her, nosed the blanket away from her back, and sniffed at the spots of blood on her legs and arms where the leeches had been. Alicia stiffened. The cat had never been this close before, and from what she knew, Tawny had not eaten tonight. The girl feared the scent of blood might cause the great cat to react.

Tawny settled down behind her and began to lick the wounds gently. Alicia tensed as the rough tongue cleaned the bites. For several long moments, she waited for sharp teeth to sink into her flesh, but when nothing more happened, she relaxed, taking comfort from the gentle washing. The cleansing soothed the itchy red bumps swollen on her skin.

Tawny stopped her ministrations and curled up against the girl's back. Alicia could feel the great rumbling breaths of the cat and closed her eyes. Tonight she would sleep safe and warm. Tomorrow, she would start what she hoped would be the last part of her journey and head southeast to the great tree. Tomorrow she would be on her way to see Gran'Tree.

The following day, Alicia and Tawny broke camp. *Well, as usual, it's* me *breaking camp,* Alicia thought as she went about her morning tasks. *Who knows where that cat got off to? Probably hunting some breakfast.*

Alicia was starving this morning after barely escaping with her life the night before. The adrenaline spike followed by the crash left little room for hunger, and she had gone to sleep without eating. She looked into her backpack and found the plastic bag with some trail mix still left in it, along with about a third of her jerky. She had been good at rationing it over the course of her journey, relying instead on what she could scavenge from the land. She finished off the last of the gorp and another couple chunks of the jerky, leaving her with roughly a quarter of what she had started out with. She put the empty trail mix bag back inside her pack. On the way, she would search for more huckleberries to fill the bag, along with pine seeds if she could find them.

"Ha! I'll make my own 'trail mix' with goodies picked up from along the trail!" Alicia laughed at her own joke. She was also sure they would find a small pond or stream with fish along the way.

Alicia had an amazing internal compass in the forest, having spent so much time exploring these woods by herself when she was younger, and she had an innate sense of direction. If she used the lake as the central point, everything else radiated out from that landmark. Even though three years had passed, she still remembered the general direction to the massive yellow pine. All she had to do was find the tallest hill on the way and scout forward. She felt sure she would be able to see the huge valley based on the distance between the mountains surrounding it. She wondered if Gran'Tree was still enormous, as he would be even easier to spot, towering high above it all.

Despite the terror and the setback of the previous day, Alicia was in good spirits. She felt surprisingly confident, given that her past three attempts at finding help ended in disappointment. And she felt an intense bonding with Tawny after the cougar had shown her such great care sleeping protectively close to Alicia's back all night. She imagined that must be what it felt like to be a kitten, cared for so tenderly.

Once she decided on her course of action, Alicia knew it was the right path. Remembering back to her last encounter with Gran'Tree, the girl recalled the strength and power that flowed through her as she sang. She hadn't felt that ever before in her life. Maybe the great tree had brought that strength to the surface. Perhaps it had been a combination of both of their powers blending together that had broken through the barrier, allowing her to go home. If they affected the barrier that way, perhaps their combined power could *heal* the barrier as well. And though she had felt the same way just a couple of days earlier when she set out to find the Ancients, this *truly* was her last hope. It had to work!

Tawny returned from wherever she had been roaming and approached the girl. "This is it, Tawny," Alicia said, hopefully. "This is the last leg of our journey. The distance is far, but we're close to being done! Are you ready?"

The large cat simply looked at her and blinked, its huge golden eyes shining. Alicia concluded over the past several days that this was Tawny's way of agreeing, or at least not being opposed to the suggestion. She grabbed her pack and hoisted it onto her back along with the fishing spear.

Alicia did a quick survey of the camping spot to make sure she didn't forget anything. She no longer had her walking stick having left it alongside the opening of the mine before going in, and she certainly hadn't stopped to pick it up when she fled.

There was absolutely no way she was going back now to retrieve it.

"Okay," she said to no one and everyone. "Let's go."

Plotting her course, Alicia decided she would curve around to the back side of the mountain just to her left and then turn east. Tawny padded alongside, her flank occasionally touching the girl's leg in a reassuring manner as if to say, *I know yesterday was bad, and I'm here for you. You are my family now.*

CH. 17 TRUE COMPANIONS

The next few days passed uneventfully. Alicia found a new walking stick; it was not perfect, but it would suffice. The two companions followed various trails, all of them headed in the general direction she felt they needed to go, which kept the duo moving at a good pace. Tawny would always wander off during the afternoons and, occasionally, Alicia heard the squeal of some creature she imagined was the great cat's prey. The girl was thankful that Tawny chose to kill her target out of sight, and understood it was only natural. She simply didn't want to see it.

When it came to food for herself, Alicia found plenty of berries along the paths and the occasional stream to keep her water bottle filled. Everything here looked so lush and vibrant, much more so than her previous visit during the time of The Drying, and even more than in her world.

Days were spent taking in all the sights and moving through large areas she had never explored before, even when hiking with her father.

Nights were quiet affairs. Alicia talked to the cougar, sharing stories of her friends at home. She described how they would ride bikes together around the neighborhood or through the local park, always stopping by the stream to see if there were frogs, but her friends didn't appreciate nature the way she did. She also talked about the sleepovers they would have. She and her friends would watch scary movies and eat pizza, screaming and laughing until her father would inevitably show up telling them, "Quiet down; it's late!" He would disappear back down the hallway to his bedroom, which re-sumed their laughter when the coast was clear, but in hushed tones.

Tawny would lay in front of Alicia, watching the girl tell stories with her head resting on two large front paws. Alicia sometimes looked at Tawny and wondered if the cougar remained with her because she had been commanded to protect her, or if she genuinely enjoyed the girl's company and felt the same connection Alicia did. She hoped it was the second option.

The cat curled up by her side each night now, her furry body hot against Alicia's side. One evening, right as she began falling asleep, she heard the distant howls of wolves and Tawny raised her head, perking her ears toward the sound, listening intently for a moment before lowering her head back onto her paws. The weary girl felt safe falling asleep like that—the cat next to her, guarding against the dangers of the night.

Alicia thought about what Vulcan had said about many of the magical forest creatures returning. The idea excited her! During the long days of walking, her eyes constantly darted around, looking for any sign of movement, hoping to catch a glimpse of a brownie or a pixie. Naturally, she wished with all her heart that she would see the unicorn, but though she saw small bushes move where there did not appear to be a squirrels, she never saw any creatures from her fantasy books. And though she occasionally heard sounds that might be the high pitched giggles of a gnome or goblin sneaking around to steal her belongings, they might also simply be the sounds of a small hidden stream, burbling through the rocks.

On the third day after leaving the Silver King, they came to a wide swamp nestled in a small valley, where water collected and had grown stagnant. Alicia looked to the sides and around the edges of the valley, but the brush there was overgrown. She decided it would be easier to traverse the swamp than to go around it.

Reluctantly, she trudged down into the valley, shoes sloshing into the water which was only inches deep. The smell of decay rose around her, noxious fumes bursting from underneath patches of fungus that grew on the still surface. It reminded her briefly of her short time in the mine, but the sun was out, and she let the memories of that encounter fade.

Amphibians, including salamanders and toads, scurried or hopped away from her feet. Small water skippers skated effortlessly across the surface, darting away from her approach.

As she moved, Alicia kept her eyes alert for giant water bugs. The large bugs liked to rest under the surface of swampy water such as this, motionless, almost invisible, waiting for their food to swim by. They were a couple of inches in length and had large front claws with which to grab their prey, using their sharp proboscises to stab their food and suck out the liquefied insides, like a spider with a fly. Normally, they ignored humans, moving quickly out of the way to avoid getting stepped on, preferring to feast on the frogs and small fish of the swamp. But if startled, their bite was painful.

Even though she wore boots, Alicia wanted to make sure she stayed clear of the bugs, especially since the experience with leeches was so fresh in her mind. She would have preferred to avoid the swamp altogether, but the tangle of brush along the sides was impossible for her to navigate effectively. She knew she was close to her destination and was eager to move quickly.

Off in the distance, along the edge of the small valley, she could see flashes of golden fur. Tawny silently searched for prey that would be her next meal but refused to get her paws wet in the dirty swamp water.

Alicia became aware of a disturbance some distance away to her right. A sudden splashing noise caused her to look, and she saw a great wriggling movement as a multitude of swamp creatures began to flee a rising mound of muddy earth.

She watched the rising sphere which looked like a dark brown bubble forming on the surface of the water. The bubble grew larger, rising and expanding, becoming a full three feet tall before ceasing its movement.

Fascinated, Alicia stepped toward the mound, waiting to see what would happen next. She heard a low growl from the bushes at the edge of the swamp behind her and turned to see the cat watching her closely.

"It's okay, Tawny," she insisted, but stopped her approach to the bubble.

Turning back to face it, she heard a wet sucking and separating noise, like dog food sliding from a can. As she watched, Alicia saw a line appear in the bubble, bisecting it from left to right. Slowly the line divided to reveal a shiny black orb of incredible size beneath—and then it blinked.

Alicia was so surprised that she stumbled backward and fell on her rump in the water. Tawny's growl grew louder, and Alicia scrambled to her feet, watching the large bulbous eye watch *her*.

She became aware of a new sound—a soggy gurgling, like water running down a bathtub drain—then saw a fleshy tentacle-like object emerge from beneath the water in front of the thing. Fully six feet in length, the tentacle was mottled pink and gray.

She watched the thing slowly sweep across the water. An almost visible stench, like that of a sewer, drifted through the air and enveloped the girl. The foul tongue-like appendage collected small creatures and fungus, which stuck to the slime that coated its surface, before retreating back into whatever mouth lay hidden from view.

Alicia was both enthralled and grossed out by what she had just witnessed. The great eye closed once more and slowly sank back into the mud, disappearing from sight. Its absence stirred the girl into motion. She turned and hurriedly stepped toward the edge of the swamp and Tawny, who waited there looking anxious. She didn't know how many more of those things lived under this murky water, or how far that disgusting tongue could reach, and she didn't want to find out. They would continue crossing the valley through the bushes along the side, regardless of how difficult that might be.

Alicia finally cleared the small depression in the valley and left the swamp behind her. By the time the sun started setting, Tawny had not yet returned from hunting for her food. With darkness falling, the sprites appeared once more, their multi-colored lights floating close by, and Alicia thought of trying to sing to them, but she couldn't remember the notes that Vulcan had used.

"Are you still watching me through their eyes?" she asked, directing the question toward the unseen Ancient. But there was no response, and, honestly, she hadn't expected one.

Suddenly, their lights began to dim rapidly. Alicia heard a noise in the brush and reached out, putting a hand on her spear. Tawny stepped into the firelight, her muzzle wet, carrying a large salmon in her jaws. She approached the girl and dropped the fish at Alicia's feet.

"You went fishing for me?" overcome with emotion, she dropped to her knees and threw her arms around the cougar's neck in a tight hug, ignoring for the moment that this creature could easily kill her.

They were past that now, and she was so thankful for the cat's presence.

Tawny tolerated the hug, and, when the girl released her, moved a few steps away and gently stretched out next to the fire. Alicia found a strong stick and skewered the salmon, giving it a little rinse first with clean water from her water bottle. She remembered thinking not so long ago that she would be grossed out by a fish with the cougar's slobber on it, but was so moved by the gesture, that thought no longer bothered her at all.

She cooked the salmon slowly over the fire, rotating the stick every few minutes. It was a large fish, more than enough for her, so she shared some with the great cat, who eagerly chewed up the leftovers, head and all.

The following day, they climbed a hill where they could see a tall tree at the summit. Reaching the peak, Alicia took off her backpack and jumped as high as she could to grab onto a low, thick branch. It was strong, and she swung her legs up like it was one of the bars in the jungle gym at her old school, using it to pull herself up into the tree.

She continued to climb, moving gracefully from one branch to the next as easily as if they were the rungs of a ladder. Carefully, she made her way higher. Eventually, the branches grew smaller and thinned out until, at last she had a view. Peering between pine needles, she scanned the horizon.

There! She could make out a larger valley that looked familiar, like it could be the right size. There weren't any similarly sized clearings that she could see, but she wasn't one hundred percent sure, and she couldn't identify the form of the great tree towering high. But maybe...

She carefully clambered down the tree and rejoined Tawny on the ground. The cat looked at her questioningly, as if she did not understand why the human had suddenly decided to behave like a squirrel.

"I think we are close," she told the cat. "I see a large valley ahead. We should reach it tomorrow or the next day at the very latest."

She crouched down at the base of the tree and pulled out the bag of huckleberries she had been collecting, eating a handful of the sweet things, then taking a long drink of water.

Stuffing the items back into her pack, she reached out and scratched the cougar between the ears. "You have been a true companion, haven't you?" she said. "I wish I could take you home with me. Not back to the city, of course. A great cat like you would never fit in there! I only mean back to my world."

She looked at the cougar fondly. "But I suppose you belong here, don't you? Away from humankind. They wouldn't understand you aren't dangerous." She paused. "Or maybe you are and I'm the one who doesn't understand. But you wouldn't hurt me, would you? Even if you were no longer under Thunderbolt's orders, you wouldn't hurt me, would you?"

Alicia stroked her hand down the cat's neck, feeling the scars where no hair grew. "You are strong and brave," she said. "You've shown me kindness—bringing me fish. And you've shown me care after my meeting with the Silver King. You are good, I can tell."

She stood once again and picked up her back-pack, turned in the direction of the valley she had seen from the limbs of the tree, and started down the other side of the hill. Boy, would she have a story to tell in her end-of-the-summer report for her future English teacher!

Almost there, she thought. *Almost there.*

CH. 18 AN OLD FRIEND

The pair followed a faint trail through the pass and entered the valley, pausing to look around and get their bearings. Alicia stared into the distance, recognizing the region, yet seeing it in an entirely new light, while Tawny prowled at her side. Ahead of them, the green valley stretched far and wide.

Life had found its way back; the clearing was absolutely filled with a variety of wildflowers. To Alicia, it was both familiar and unfamiliar. She imagined this must have been what it looked like eons ago when the Ancient Ones gathered here to work their terrible magics—except for one big difference.

In the middle of the meadow stood Gran'Tree, waiting. She was sure he could see them even now and at this distance. She also felt sure he knew who it was that approached his meadow.

Alicia gazed down along the trail they traveled to where it met the floor of the valley, and her breath hitched in her throat. A long-forgotten memorial to a giant friend stood there, resting among the multitude of flowers that surrounded it. Slowly, she strode down the path and, reaching the base, moved forward and approached the remains of Bristleback.

Four thousand years of time and weather had reduced the great mountain troll to nothing more than a large hill of sand. Moving to the edge, Alicia set aside her walking stick and sank to her knees, stretching forward. She dug both hands into the great pile before her, feeling the residual warmth of the day still trapped within the sand soaking into her fingers and palms.

Resting her hands in the remnants of her once-giant friend, Alicia's thoughts returned to her previous visit and how terrified she had been of the troll when her group had first stumbled upon him. They literally stumbled upon him and ended up on his enormous back without realizing it.

Alicia had been sure she was going to die at that moment, with her friends surrounding her, torn apart and eaten by the monster, her bones ground to dust by the terrible stone teeth. To her surprise, she found common ground with the massive creature. Like her, Bristleback had been separated from his kind, and in his loneliness, he let his anger rule him. Faced with this young, strong-willed girl and his own looming mortality, he chose to help them on the last leg of their journey, ultimately collapsing here—his final resting place—his huge body rapidly turning to stone as she and her companions watched tearfully. He was the last of the mountain trolls in this region, taken by The Drying just moments before salvation.

These memories brought an unexpected flood of tears. Alicia withdrew her hands, carrying small piles of sand cupped in her palms.

She watched the fine grains absorb her tears, which fell in large droplets, splashing onto the remains of her friend.

"Oh, Bristleback! You were so misunderstood, yet so kind," she sobbed. "You shared the last moments of your life with me, a gift I could never repay. Where are you now? Do you know that I made it home to my parents? Do you know that, with your help, I saved these lands?" She chuckled ruefully through her tears. "It turns out I may have broken them as well—the barrier at least. Not on purpose, of course. And not directly, either. It was Gran'Tree who weakened it. But I helped in my own way. I didn't know I had that kind of power." Alicia smiled, wiping away her tears. "But you did, didn't you? You said so, I remember."

Alicia remembered back to that day when she last set foot in this valley. "I told Mickey," she said to the pile of sand, "I told Mickey, Briar, and Fiona that I was going to ask Gran'Tree to send me home, just like you suggested I should. You were right. They were my family and they needed to know my plans. And I made it home!"

She began to sob again and the big cat came to her side, leaning against her gently, giving unspoken support. "They are gone now, all of them. Everybody's gone, including you. So much time has passed—thousands of years. To me, it seems like it could have been just the other day!"

Alicia stared into the sand cupped in her hands. She was a little girl once again reliving the tragedy of that day, tears streaming uncontrollably down her cheeks. Spreading her fingers slowly, she watched the small grains of sand fall away. It was like watching an hourglass as what remained of her huge friend slipped back into the pile in front of her.

Like an hourglass. The mental image reminded her of this current quest and what was at stake—her parents trapped in time. The fractures that must be sealed. How many more people or creatures were trapped as well?

Alicia slowly rubbed her hands together, brushing away the last of the sand, and looked at Bristleback's remains. "And now I'm back," she said, choking back the sobs, the remaining tears slowly drying on her face. "Surprise!" She smiled again, a small, sad smile. "The barrier is cracked and the years have further weakened it. Now your time is bubbling over into my world. My parents are trapped—frozen solid—and I need to find a way to fix this."

Alicia raised her eyes and stared off at the great tree in the distance. She knew he was watching her, and she resented being seen during this brief time of mourning.

"I wish you were here, Bristleback. I could use your advice again." With the sun in her eyes, it was hard to see the details of the yellow pine, but she remembered what he looked like years ago.

"I met with the Ancient Ones," she told the troll. "I don't know if you ever met them during your long life. I thought that since they created the barrier, they could help repair it." She dropped her gaze to the ground, remembering the joy and hope she felt then. "Vulcan seemed to be the most interested, but she and Thunderbolt only used me for their own purposes." Her eyes, no longer filled with tears, were fiery and focused. "The Silver King was terrible!

They all abused their power and have yet to recover. Who knows if they ever will?" Looking back at the tree, she lamented, "And now I have to meet with *him*." She spoke the last word low, drawing it out, showing her disdain for what she had to do.

Alicia looked back at the massive pile of sand that was once the mountain troll and let out a long sigh. Slowly, she rose to her feet, with Tawny at her side.

"I'm sure wherever you are, it's better than here. I hope you are with friends. I hope you are with family." She looked at the remains of her friend a moment longer. "I miss you."

Turning away, she looked again into the distance. Reaching down, she stroked the great cat's head, taking comfort in her presence. "Let's get this over with," she said. The tree ahead of her was her last chance. She just hoped there were no hard feelings.

CH. 19 GRAN'TREE REVISITED

Alicia walked through the field of flowers, letting her hands brush along tall stems as she moved. She inhaled the myriad of light and aromatic scents that hung in the air.

The last time she was here, the surrounding lands were barren and dry, with wild dust devils spinning their way across the empty soil. Now the valley was filled with green grasses and wildflowers of all colors. Beautiful oranges and reds of paint-brush and poppies contrasted with the white of the Syringa flowers. As she moved through the tall vegetation, dusty green grasshoppers and yellow butterflies took flight around her.

Alicia approached the great tree with caution and was amazed at the transformation. Gran'Tree, once enormous and frightening, now appeared very much like any other tree in the woods. Alicia felt taken aback by the sight of him. He still towered high in the valley but held none of his terrible former glory. Even so, the girl still felt some of her old fear return. After all, the last time she set eyes on this being, he was filled with strength, which he had converted into his own dark power, stolen from all the living creatures of the surrounding lands.

As Alicia drew closer to the yellow pine, she could see the toll that thousands of years had taken on the tree. The tree's skin was old, the bark appeared shriveled, like her fingers after swimming or an apple left out in the sun for too long. There was a large scattering of the distinctive puzzle piece-like shapes that made up his bark surrounding the base of the tree.

Alicia looked up into his face and saw eyes dimmed by time. The moss surrounding the eye-lids, once bright green, was now brown and dark. The frozen rivers of sap around his mouth had grown long, a sign of the tree's life force draining away over the ages.

Those dim eyes now looked down at the girl walking toward him. "Iiii reeemmeeemmbeeerrr youuu, liiittllle ooonnne. Yooouuu'rrre noooot sooo liiittllle aaanyyymooorrre," Gran'Tree grumbled low and soft as she approached. The strength of his voice, which once boomed across the land, was now reduced to barely more than a whisper. "Haaavvve youuu reeetuuurrrnnned affffteeerrr aaalll thiiisss tiiimmme tooo loook upooonnn meee wiiith piiityyy aaat whaaat Iiii haaavvve beeecooommme?"

Alicia and the cat reached the base, and she looked up at Gran'Tree, surprised to find that she felt sorrow for the great tree, even after all the destruction he'd wrought. To see a being fall from such majesty created a feeling of mortality that almost overwhelmed her. If such a creature of power could be reduced to the husk of its former self, what were all our lives but moments of time? Everyone she had known here in the Wild Side was gone. Only Gran'Tree remained, and he appeared weakened beyond belief.

The trials of her journey came crashing down around her—everything she had done, the Ancients she had talked to—it all came flooding back. She had power. They all sensed it. Why couldn't *she*? No matter how hard she searched herself for something special, she came away feeling utterly human.

She could feel it staring her in the face, but she was too blind to see it. Where had the young girl of just a few years ago gone, so full of excitement, with a thirst for adventure? Why had her focus turned away from the magic of these woods, her cabin, and the lake, lost to the pressures of the approaching school year and the new challenges she would face? She couldn't even remember the words to the songs she used to sing with her father. She couldn't remember the song she had sung to Gran'Tree!

Surely she could have struck a better balance for her life, but she had made no effort to do so. Now she found there was barely time to swim with her parents. Certainly, she may be too big to get launched from her father's shoulders, but she shouldn't have put simple things aside like floating lazily on an inner tube in the lake. Walking the trails and exploring the wilderness had shaped her into the young woman she was today.

These feelings crushed her. Alicia remembered her adventures in these woods just a few short years ago. She loved this forest more than anything. Alicia remembered her parents taking her on afternoon picnics to the hot springs, or down to the river, searching for salamanders under the large rocks while her father stood knee-deep in the cold water casting out a fishing line. She was also flooded with memories of learning so many little things about the wilds from her mother. She had let those feeling slip away. She had let that *magic* slip away. And now it was buried deep beneath schoolwork and friends who felt make-believe was for children.

At that moment, staring up at what remained of the most powerful being she had ever met, even at her young age Alicia truly understood that life could be fleeting. She made a promise to herself that, if she made it through this journey and found a way to save her family, she would live the rest of her life with more zeal, help others, and take pleasure in all the small details each and every day.

Spending much more time with her parents was suddenly important too. Friends her age would grow with her, but her parents were farther down the path of life, like Gran'Tree. Why had she not realized this before? She wouldn't turn away from her studies and education, not at all, but she would find the balance she needed to keep all this magic in her life.

"No, Gran'Tree, I have not come to mock you," Alicia said sadly, no longer having to raise her voice to be heard by the being in front of her. "I don't feel happy about what's happened to you."

"Theeennn whyyy dooo youuu reeetuuurrrnnn afffteeerrr sooo looonnng?" the tree asked.

"It's because of my parents. You cracked the barrier between the realms. Actually, *we* cracked the barrier—you with your great roots and me by weakening you and causing your roots to shrink. Now my parents are trapped."

Alicia explained to the great tree all that had happened and all that she had learned, beginning with walking out of her cabin and seeing her mother frozen in time and her father going to investigate.

The great tree listened patiently to the story. When she was done, Alicia asked with the last bit of hope she could muster, "Can you help me?"

"Youuu haaavvve theee maaagiiic," Gran'Tree answered.

"I don't know how to use it anymore!" Alicia exclaimed. "It's lost, buried. I've forgotten!" She looked to the great tree. "You saw me use it. You are the only one left who has felt it. Please, help me find it again," she begged.

"Youuu diiidnnn't loooossse iiit," the yellow pine said. "Youuu leeeft iiit heeerrrre. Iit haaasss beeennn waaaiiitiiinnng heeerrre fooorrr youuu tooo reetuuurrrnnn." Gran'Tree's voice rumbled low and eager in his throat. "Heeerrre, beneeeaath theee ssskiinnn Iiii sheeed."

Alicia had no idea what the being could be talking about. She looked down at the base of the tree and saw nothing—only piles of bark fallen from the tree as it aged. What could Gran'Tree possibly mean? She had not left anything behind here.

"I don't see anything!" she said in frustration, her eyes searching every inch of soil around his trunk. "I didn't leave anything here!"

"Ooohhh, buuut youuu diiid. Youuuurrr staaaff ooofff poooweeerrr. Looook theeerrre."

Alicia looked again. There was no staff! But—wait. There *was* something different there. Something separate, underneath the puzzle piece-like bark. What was that?

Alicia knelt down and began to dig, casting aside handfuls of the old bark, creating a hole. She continued to brush away the fallen pieces, slowly uncovering and revealing what lay below. *Oh my gosh!* She saw what lay there and remembered.

The young girl stepped out onto the porch of the cabin. Her father was already waiting for her, dressed in his jeans, a flannel shirt, and hiking boots. "Are you ready?" he asked.

The five-year-old girl had shoulder-length blonde hair and freckles, and wore a pair of tattered overalls. They had been new and clean just a couple months earlier, but she liked to climb rocks and explore, so there were more than a few rips in the material.

She and her father were getting ready to go on one of their weekly hikes. Always eager to find out what new and hidden location he would lead her to, she looked forward to these moments. She absolutely *lived* to discover new places.

"Ready!" she exclaimed, jumping recklessly down the two stone steps in front of their cabin. Her philosophy, if she could have one at such a young age, was why do things the easy way when the hard way was more fun?

Before leaving, they moved off underneath the nearby trees and began their search, always part of the ritual of the day. The first task was to find an old tree branch that was just the right length and weight. Her dad would then use his carving knife to transform it into the perfect walking stick.

"A good walking stick is key," her dad would tell her. "It can be used to help support you when the trail is rough or to test the depth of water when you needed to cross a small stream. It can also be used to move a branch aside that might scratch you. And in the end, it can mark where you've been."

She especially liked that last part. Whenever they would reach their final destination, the girl and her father would take their sticks and stab them into the ground or between a pair of rocks to signify the accomplishment of reaching their goal. She imagined that throughout these woods, hikers might stumble across a pair of sticks poking out of the ground, one tall and one short, and wonder how they had gotten there.

As the girl grew older, she continued to go on hikes, sometimes with her father and sometimes alone. Every time, she would go through the ritual of finding a walking stick that brought her joy, and it always kept her company when her father couldn't join her. The walking stick was a symbol of happiness and love to the girl. Holding it firmly in her hand gave her a sense of power and confidence.

When she was eleven years old, the girl got lost in a rainstorm. She was confused and alone, except for a woodland creature that had found her. She knew she had a journey ahead of her to find her way home, but before she got started, the experienced hiker knew what she needed to make.

Alicia pushed aside the fallen bark, uncovering the rest of the object underneath. It was her old walking stick, the one she had first found and used on her journey to this valley, so many years ago! She had dropped it here. It was incredible to see that it still remained intact at the base of the giant tree, after all this time.

Alicia reached out to pick up the walking stick. When she did, she felt a powerful thrum of energy course through her hand and up her arm like an electric shock. Her body stiffened, and she forced her fingers to open, quickly dropping the stick.

"What is this?" she asked Gran'Tree.

"Iiit iiisss youuurrr maaagiiic. Iiit iiisss youuurrr poooweeerrr," he boomed, his voice becoming stronger. "Durrriiinnng youuurrr traaaveeelll, iiit dreeewww poooweeerrr frooommm youuu. Wheeennn youuu saaannng, iiit absooorrrbed youuurrr streeennngth. Oveeerrr theee aaageesss, iiitsss poooweeerrr haaasss grrrooowwwnnn. Taaake iiit!" he urged.

Alicia reached out again, picking up the stick once more. This time, knowing what to expect, she held on with all her might, almost welcoming the surge of energy she felt emanating from it. She felt her body stiffening again and worked to relax herself and allow the power to flow through her, not control her.

"Taaake youuurr staaafff. Reeetuuurrrnnn tooo youuurr moootheerrr aaannnd faaatheeer- rr. Smaaash theee baaarrrieeerrr aaannnd freee theeemmm. Thiiisss youuu muuussst dooo aaan- nd youuu wiiilll beee reeeunnniiiteeed."

Alicia got the feeling that the yellow pine was not telling her everything, but she could feel strong mag- ic within the walking stick. It had petrified over the millennia and felt more like stone in her grasp. Her hand found the smooth indentation worn into the surface so long ago by her young grip. It felt smaller beneath her fingers, which were much longer now, and she squeezed it tightly.

The feeling was incredible, and it filled her with strength. Alicia stood, the newfound energy flowing through her, reinvigorating her muscles and seemingly sharpening her mind. Music filled her head, the songs of her youth blending with the voice she remembered from Vulcan. For the first time in her life, she was truly aware of how it felt to have magic. The feeling was amazing! It was euphoric. She was drunk on it and reveled in the feeling. This was the key; she was sure of it. She could return to her world and free her parents from the time distortion.

She looked up at Gran'Tree. "Thank you," she said gratefully, but the words came out in song. The great tree visibly flinched back from the notes the girl sang, his branches trembling. She saw his reaction and said no more.

Turning away from the tree, she noticed Tawny pacing rapidly back and forth, a worried look on her face. She crouched and whispered to the cat. "It's okay. Everything is going to be okay now." The musical notes of her words seemed to soothe the cougar.

Ready to go home, Alicia cast a final look in Gran'Tree's direction and then began walking back toward the entrance to the valley, her new staff in hand, enjoying the sensations coming from deep within the petrified wood. She quickened her steps effortlessly as if she had just awoken from a long nap. She was full of renewed energy. There was no time to waste; she had found what she was looking for.

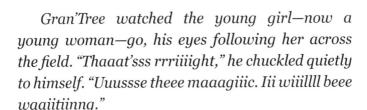

Gran'Tree watched the young girl—now a young woman—go, his eyes following her across the field. "Thaaat'sss rrriiiight," he chuckled quietly to himself. "Uuussse theee maaagiiic. Iii wiiillll beee waaiitiinng."

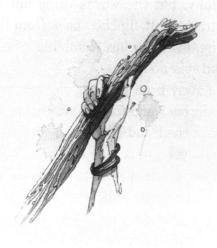

CH. 20 THE BREAKING

Alicia let her hand slide down the staff, feeling the smooth wood that had been revealed when the bark was worn away long ago. She gripped it firmly at the base with both hands, the knots there dully jabbing into her palms.

The trek back to Moose Beach, to that passage from one realm to the other, had taken days. Still, Alicia's mood remained bright and filled with excitement. She sang every day, feeling crackles of energy travel across her skin like electricity as she did. It didn't matter what song, it didn't even matter if there were words or not. She had found her magic! Alicia didn't yet know of the powers it gave her or what, exactly, she could use it for. But after what Gran'Tree had said, she was sure that she could smash the bubble of time and free her parents, which was the only thing that mattered right now.

Tawny seemed happier too, more playful in the way she bounded through the brush. Perhaps she picked up on Alicia's mood, or perhaps she was charmed by the singing. But the golden-eyed cat appeared to be very cautious of the girl's staff. In the evenings, she waited until Alicia put the staff away before curling up next to her. The power it wielded was unknown, and to the cat, unknown often meant dangerous, and perhaps it was.

On the first afternoon with the staff, Alicia walked along the path, mindlessly snapping her fingers along to the rhythm of a song when, suddenly, her hand spontaneously caught fire. Confused and terrified, she fled to a nearby stream to put it out. When her panic receded, it slowly dawned on her that she had not felt any pain while her hand was on fire. So she tried it again, vigorously snapping her fingers, then watching the orange flames lick across her fingers before shaking her hand to extinguish them. What a wonderful find!

It was an aspect of the staff's magic that Alicia had not discovered before, but it came in handy while making camp in the evenings. She could summon the small flame on her fingertips which she could use to light the campfire more quickly than with the matches.

When she and Tawny finally neared the lake-shore and Alicia's invisible passage home, she dropped to her knees and once again wrapped the cougar's neck in a tight hug. The cat seemed more patient with it this time and nuzzled into the girl's hair as if she wanted to smell the human one last time to remember her.

"I love you, Tawny," Alicia cried softly. "Be good. Don't bite anyone. Well, unless they're mean." She reached up and stroked the animal's scarred neck. "And stay away from whatever gave you these. I want you to live a long and happy life."

She pulled away from the cougar and sat looking into those golden eyes. "I love you," she said again. "Be safe."

The great cat slowly blinked her tawny-colored eyes at the girl. And with that, Alicia stood and walked toward the lakeshore, equal parts hesitant to leave her new friend and anxious to free her parents.

She felt the resistance of the barrier again this time, but did not have to work to find her way to cross. She could see the outline of her boat like it was a ghost, as if it tried to exist in this world but was not quite there. Singing, she stepped forward. The sensation of a strong wind resisted her movements only for a moment, and then she was through.

The colors around her faded, the light dimmed a bit, and the air turned colder. Otherwise, it looked exactly the same, and now the fully formed boat floated just ahead, waiting right where she left it as if only a few minutes had passed. When she stopped to think, Alicia realized that was the truth! She had traveled for weeks in the Wild Side, but here in her realm, only fifteen or twenty minutes had gone by since she left.

She quickly untied the rowboat and jumped in carefully, laying the staff and her pack on the floor of the boat alongside her. She was eager to get back across the lake, but took the time to put on her life jacket again. She didn't know if being able to breathe underwater would be one of the new powers her staff granted her, but she wasn't willing to risk it.

Placing the oars in the oarlocks, she turned the boat around and paddled swiftly. Alicia watched the receding shoreline of Moose Beach, no longer able to see Tawny. She hoped the big cat would be okay and wondered if she would return to Thunderbolt. She knew the cat didn't belong to him, but perhaps it would seek out human companionship though the old man was rather sour and she didn't know if he would be good company at all. Maybe it would be different for the cat.

As she rowed, she saw frozen bubbles, the same ones she had seen weeks ago. Or had it only been minutes? How should she refer to time? It was all very confusing.

Reaching her dock, Alicia grabbed the staff and tossed it on the shore. She gently stepped out of the boat so as not to capsize it and tied it to the old stump. She stripped off the life jacket, threw it into the boat, scooped up the staff, and ran up the hill.

Alicia stood behind her cabin, gripping the staff at its base, her parents frozen in front of her. She held the stick out straight and lined it up with the edge of the time sphere closest to her.

She looked at her parents, motionless within the bubble. Questions ran rapidly through her mind. *Were they aware? Could they sense time passing outside while their bodies remained trapped inside? Had the clockworks of their minds stopped just as completely as their hands, fingers, and eyes? Would the actions she was about to take hurt them? Were they even alive anymore, or had they died, locked in there forever, a tragic reminder of the damage she had helped cause?*

With that last thought, Alicia planted her feet firmly in the dirt and lifted the walking stick over her shoulder like a baseball player gearing up for a home run. *Please let this work*, was her final thought, a plea to God and to the Ancients of the other realm. Alicia began to sing, feeling the energy running up the staff, through her arms and body, coalescing around her.

When she felt ready, Alicia swung with all her might.

The staff struck the sphere with a tremendous *CRAAACKKK!* that reverberated through the air. The sound of a thousand crystal chandeliers falling simultaneously onto a thousand tile floors exploded outward, expanding rapidly through the forest, across the lake, and over the hills beyond. Alicia dropped the remains of the now shattered staff to the ground and threw her hands over her ears, closing her eyes against the onslaught of noise. It sounded like the very universe was breaking into a million pieces.

After what seemed like countless, long, drawn-out seconds, the great crashing faded to echoes bouncing around the mountains surrounding the lake.

"That sounds like quite some thunder! We'd better get inside before the storm hits." It was her mother's voice.

Alicia slowly opened her eyes. There in front of her stood her parents, her father's hand resting on her mother's shoulder, both looking quizzically at her.

"Alicia, are you okay?" her father asked.

The girl stared at her parents a moment longer before throwing herself at them, almost knocking them over with the ferocity of her hug.

"Hey, hey, hey!" her father chuckled. "What's all that for?"

"You're okay! You're alive, and you're okay!" Alicia exclaimed through tears of joy.

"And why wouldn't we be?" her mother asked, hugging the girl back.

"I've got so much to tell you," Alicia said, pulling away and looking at them.

"Did you finish your repor—" her father stopped mid-sentence, looking off into the distance. "What is that?" he asked, a note of awe in his voice.

Alicia became aware of a new sound and turned to look toward the lake where her father was facing. She froze and her mouth slowly fell open. Out on the water, what looked like a mighty wind rapidly blew across the surface from the other side, pushing ahead of it a massive wave tipped with whitecaps. She had never seen anything like it.

The wave came fast and crashed viciously against the shoreline, shaking their dock as if it were made of popsicle sticks, and leaving behind dozens of fish, wet and flopping on the shore, under the afternoon sun. The wind continued pushing ahead, up the slope toward them, bending branches and small trees as it came.

"Look out!" Richard screamed and threw his arms around his wife and daughter. He spun them both away from the wind, shielding them from the gale and the debris it carried with it. Pine needles, dirt, and fallen bark pelted his back and arms, leaving small scratches behind.

The wind rushed past them and continued on into the forest. Richard slowly released his grip on his family, and together they looked around in wonder. Everything looked...*different*...changed. It was as if there had been a haze in the air that the passing wind had blown away. Everything looked brighter, more vivid, and bursting with color, Alicia thought. The same way things appeared in the...*oh no*...what had she done?

Alicia looked down at the broken and splintered staff lying discarded on the ground. She had power, she knew that now. Three years ago, when she had crossed the barrier, her actions had helped create the cracks. And now...

Looking up, she surveyed the woods around her. "The colors look brighter and more vivid," she said, continuing the thought out loud. "The same way they looked in the Wild Side."

"Alicia, what are you talking about?" her father asked.

The girl didn't say anything, and a cold realization washed over her, the same way the wind-whipped lake had just crashed upon their dock. She had destroyed the barrier. Once weakened by Gran'Tree, her magic had now shattered it to pieces. The realms were no longer separate. The magic had come to her world. *Smash the barrier,* he had said. Gran'Tree had *told* her what would happen, but she had only been half-listening. Her first thought had been for her family and herself. The magic of the staff and the feeling it gave her had consumed her.

Of course, given what she knew now, she would have made the same choice every time. When it came to her family, there was no choice. Had she just been a puppet all along, guided by some unseen hand? And if so, who was pulling the strings?

The words from a barely remembered dream came back to her once again. *Cooome fiiinnd meee!* She had found him, she realized. And Alicia had done exactly what he wanted.

There was a sudden movement in the forest. Richard saw it before Alicia or her mother did, and he stepped toward it, placing himself between this new threat and the girls, shouting and waving his arms frantically.

"Get away, get away!" he yelled. "Alicia, Katie, look out!"

Alicia turned in the direction he was looking and saw a great beast moving toward them. She recognized two parallel scars. Scratches running down the side of a neck. She side-stepped around her father who tried to grab her as she went past, the word "no" getting caught in his throat.

Alicia knelt, and the great cat came to her, rubbing its large face against Alicia's, before looking up at the adults. She scratched the cougar on her head. Turning back toward her parents, she saw the fear and horror on their faces.

"Mom, Dad. I'd like you to meet Tawny."

EPILOGUE

His plan succeeded. The young girl—now grown but still naive—had forgotten his former strength and underestimated his desire. He called to her and she came running like an obedient child. And because of her innocence and ignorance, the barrier was smashed!

"Sooo muuuch liiife. Sooo muuuch eeennneeer-rrgyyyy. Sooo muuuch waaateeerrr! Iiii caaannn liiivvve... agaaainnn."

Below the surface of the earth, the worms and beetles crawling their way through the dirt became aware of a slight vibration. At first, it was gentle enough to be almost unnoticeable, but it built slowly in intensity. Unseen to eyes above ground, giant roots—long thought dormant—began to stretch and reach. Searching, they sensed the large body of water far to the north and descended upon the prize.

And upon the humans that lived there.

CPSIA information can be obtained
at www.ICGtesting.com
Printed in the USA
BVHW040825101120
592416BV00013B/17/J